gender
Blender

blake
nelson

delacortepress

Published by Delacorte Press
an imprint of Random House Children's Books
a division of Random House, Inc.
New York

Delecorte Press and colophon are registered trademarks of Random House, Inc.

www.randomhouse.com/kids

Educators and librarians, for a variety of teaching tools, visit us at
www.randomhouse.com/teachers

ALLOYENTERTAINMENT

Library of Congress Cataloging-in-Publication Data

Nelson, Blake.
Gender blender / Blake Nelson.
p. cm.
Summary: When the students in health class at George Wilson Middle School are assigned girl/boy partners to discuss gender issues, no one could imagine that two students would actually switch bodies.
ISBN 0-385-74696-2 (hardcover)—ISBN 0-385-90937-3 (Gibraltar lib. bdg.)
[1. Middle schools—Fiction. 2. Schools—Fiction. 3. Sex role—Fiction.]
I. Title.
PZ7.N4328Gen 2006
[Fic]—dc22
2005014792

The text of this book is set in 12-point Goudy.

Printed in the United States of America

10 9 8 7 6 5 4 3 2 1

First Edition

BVG

FOR IONE BARROWS,
WHO EXPLAINED THINGS

Many thanks: Ben Schrank, Claudia Gabel, Josh Bank, Leslie Morgenstein, Wendy Loggia, Beverly Horowitz, and all the wonderful people at Alloy Entertainment and Random House Children's Books. And special thanks to Beth Rosenberg for helping in every way.

BASEBALL IN THE RAIN

It was a wet, drizzly morning in Seattle, Washington. Tom Witherspoon stood on the pitcher's mound at George Wilson Middle School, where he and some other people were playing a pickup baseball game before class. Tom had just struck out Zach Leland, who was throwing his usual tantrum.

"That wasn't fair!" Zach complained. "I wasn't ready!"

"Yes, you were, you wuss!" yelled the first baseman.

"*You're* the wuss!" Zach said, throwing down his bat.

"Sit down and let someone else have a turn!" the third baseman shouted.

Tom tugged on the bill of his perfectly worn Mariners cap. Across the field, several girls, including his neighbor Emma Baker, sat on a bench behind third base. That was where they spent their mornings, whispering, giggling, and

1

doing whatever it was sixth-grade girls did. He and Emma had hung out when they were little kids. But now she was a member of Courtney Hall's clique, the Grrlzillas. Tom wasn't sure what the point of Grrlzillas was, except to be incredibly annoying. Maybe they had no point. Either way, Tom wished they would sit somewhere else—they were making him nervous.

Thwack. Tom slapped the ball in his glove. Still no batter. He watched Emma chattering away. The summer before fourth grade, the two of them had built a tree fort and spent countless hours in it. They would wake up early and ride their bikes around the neighborhood. Hike on the scrubby path alongside the stream next to the park and collect bugs and cool rocks. That was ancient history now.

Finally, a new batter appeared. Great. It was Jane Hennessey. Tom was not happy to see her. Jane was a tall, athletic seventh grader who had been known to hit the ball out of the park. Way out.

"Hey, Tom!" Zach yelled from the backstop. "Think you can strike out a girl?"

"I struck you out, didn't I?" Tom yelled back. He pulled down the bill of his cap so that it covered his eyes. He had practiced his pitching all winter in hopes of making the junior Little League team this spring. If he couldn't get a few fastballs past Jane Hennessey . . . well, that would be bad.

"Whaddaya waiting for? Throw it!" Zach cried.

Jane grinned, took a few practice swings, and waited for the pitch.

Tom stared at home plate. His dad had worked with him

that Saturday and had shown him how to place his pitches. Tom tried to remember what his father had said about tall hitters. You pitched them low and outside. Or was it low and *inside*? Tom had trouble remembering details, especially under pressure. Whatever. He just needed to focus. He *had* to strike Jane out.

"C'mon! Throw it!" shouted the first baseman. "The bell's going to ring."

Tom took aim, wound up, and threw his best fastball. Jane lunged forward and whacked it toward third base. At that very moment, the third baseman was sharing his Skittles with the shortstop. Neither saw the ball as it shot past them.

"Hey!" Tom screamed. "Get that!"

The third baseman turned helplessly as the ball rolled into the outfield. He looked at Tom and shrugged.

Tom sprinted after the ball himself—he was medium height, thin, and one of the faster boys in his class. He used all his speed now. Under *no circumstances* could Jane Hennessey hit an inside-the-park home run off him.

The ball rolled to where Emma and her friends sat on their bench and stopped at Courtney Hall's feet. Tom ran to it, reached for it . . . and then Courtney kicked it.

"Don't touch that!" Tom tried again, but another girl knocked it from his grasp with her heel. The ball rolled beneath the bench and Tom dove under Margaret Cooper to get it. Unfortunately, Margaret was wearing a skirt.

"Hey!" shrieked Margaret. She was especially touchy about boys. Two days earlier, Tom's best friend, Brad Hailey,

3

had snuck up behind her in gym class and yanked down her sweatpants in front of everyone.

"What are you doing?" Margaret yelped. "Get out! Get away from me!"

Tom was caught in the skirt and fought to untangle himself. He *had* to find that ball. He could not let Jane Hennessey hit a home run.

"Perv alert! Perv alert!" Courtney shouted. She and the Grrlzillas rushed to defend Margaret. Rachel Simms kicked Tom in the butt and hit him with her backpack. The other girls joined in, whacking Tom with textbooks, gym bags, whatever they had. One of them even jabbed him with an umbrella.

"Stop it!" Tom grabbed the ball and jumped to his feet. "I was *trying* to get the ball." He turned to Emma. "Emma, help me out."

But she frowned and crossed her arms.

Tom suddenly saw Jane Hennessey rounding third. He ran clear of the girls and threw the ball as hard as he could. It was too late. Jane jogged home easily. As a final humiliation, Courtney lobbed a Hello Kitty key chain at Tom's head. "Skirt perv!" she called.

Tom muttered under his breath as Jane high-fived her teammates.

"The things a boy will do to look up a girl's dress." Rachel shook her head.

"I was getting the *ball*," Tom said, his teeth clenched. "You guys were too busy yapping to notice, but Jane was going to score!"

Margaret snorted. "Yeah, right."

Tom threw up his hands. "You got me. This whole game was played so that I could look at Margaret's flowered underwear."

Ashley Orendorfer, another Grrlzilla, rolled her eyes. "Pathetic." Emma gave him a look of pure disgust.

Courtney slung her backpack over her shoulder. "Listen up, Spoonie. We're sick of boys getting away with stuff like this. S-I-C-K. From now on, *we're* doing stuff to *you*. So get used to it."

And with that, the Grrlzillas lifted their chins and defiantly marched up the hill to school.

EMMA'S NICKNAME

Emma Baker stood at her locker and unloaded her heavy backpack, which was always weighed down with textbooks, folders, index cards, and five-subject notebooks. She had also stuffed in her gymnastics clothes, her sheet music for piano lessons, and a bunch of Girl Scout cookie flyers she was supposed to pass out at lunchtime. The bell for first period was about to ring and she hadn't dug out her glitter pen yet. She frantically rummaged through her backpack and prayed she hadn't lost it.

Actually, Emma did *everything* frantically these days. It seemed the older she got, the more stressful her schedule became. Most of it was her mother's doing. Mrs. Baker had never met an activity she didn't like. Emma enjoyed gymnastics, piano lessons, Girl Scouts, and all the other after-school things she did. It was just that she liked doing nothing every now and then too.

The bell sounded and Courtney joined Emma at her locker so they could walk to first period together.

"Can you believe Tom?" Courtney said, annoyed. "What a perv!"

Courtney stressed Emma out too. Emma still wasn't sure she fit in with the Grrlzillas. She didn't really have a problem with boys. They never did anything bad to her. But Tom was a different story. He was definitely getting on her bad side. The previous summer, Tom had suddenly refused to let her into the tree fort they had built together before fourth grade. He and Brad Hailey had told her that it was now a boys-only "chill house" and they didn't want any girl "mushiness" around. The memory of Tom and his friends laughing and pushing her away gave Emma an instant stomachache.

"Yeah, he's kind of a pain," she replied.

"Remember the Grrlzilla motto," Courtney said, flipping her hair back. "Not all boys are pervs, but all pervs are boys. Right?"

"I guess," Emma said.

Just before they reached health class, Jeff Matthews appeared in the hallway. Jeff was extremely good-looking. He wore expensive sneakers, a down vest, cargoes, and a white shell necklace that showed off the tan he'd gotten during spring break in San Diego. Emma had a huge crush on him, just like every other sixth-grade girl.

"Oh my God," Emma whispered. "Why does Jeff have to be so cute?"

Courtney gave Emma a nudge. "Go talk to him."

7

"No, no, no," Emma said, checking her shirt. She had just bought her first bra at Nordstrom and couldn't tell if it looked right.

"You gotta say something to him," Courtney said in that authoritative way she had. "Or he'll never notice you."

"I know, I know," Emma said. "It's just, he's so . . . cool. And I'm so—"

"Busy?" Courtney said.

Emma gave her a nasty look.

"Uh-oh," Courtney murmured. "Now Sienna Jones is hanging all over him."

"What are they talking about?"

"Lip gloss, probably," Courtney said. "That's all Sienna Jones ever talks about."

Emma looked closely at Jeff and tried to get her confidence up. If she could juggle all her other activities, why couldn't she juggle him? She just needed to think of him as a project. "Maybe I'll talk to him at the gymnastics meet on Saturday. His sister is on the team and he always comes to watch her."

"He comes to check out girls in their leotards, you mean," Courtney said.

Emma frowned. "Do you think he's really like that?"

"Hel-*lo*?"

"I don't care," Emma said, ignoring Courtney's raised eyebrows. "I still like him."

As she approached the classroom, Emma looked down at her chest again. She had a typical gymnast's body— small and thin. Her mom was always saying that every-

8

thing about her was cute and petite. She felt like an elf next to Courtney, who was much taller and more developed. Even though it was mildly insulting, Emma thought she'd much rather have Courtney's nickname—Queen Kong—than the one Tom and Brad had given her. How could anyone as cool as Jeff Matthews like someone called Toadstool?

HEALTH CLASS

Tom hurried to health, his first-period class. He was sweaty, muddy, and depressed. The Jane Hennessey home-run fiasco played over and over in his brain like a warped CD. He collapsed into the desk behind Brad and they did their usual handshake: shake, grip, point, high-five, low-five. Then Brad went back to drawing a naked picture of their new music teacher, Ms. O'Connor.

"Check this out," Brad said.

Tom looked at the sketch. "Yeah, that's all right, but you wanna see something really cool? Check *this* out." He felt around in his pocket and pulled out a flat stone arrowhead. He handed it to Brad.

"Wow. Where'd you find this?"

"Last night in the woods. I think it's Klickitat. Look at the writing on the other side."

Brad flipped it over. There were strange markings on the back. "These look like little pictures or something."

"It's probably an ancient message."

"It probably says *Made in Taiwan*."

"No way." Tom took the arrowhead back and slipped it in his pocket. "This thing is valuable. I'm going to sell it on eBay."

"All right, class, let's settle in," said Ms. Andre.

Brad and Tom turned forward in their seats. They liked Ms. Andre. She had a warm smile and wore her long black hair in a French braid. She was also funny, and on the first day of school she made everyone say "penis." Even the girls.

Then the door opened and Jeff Matthews came in.

"Look who decided to honor us with his presence," Brad said.

Tom watched as Jeff sauntered in. All the sixth-grade girls had crushes on him. Even Ms. Andre cut him extra slack.

"If that was us, we'd get detention," Brad muttered.

"Okay, everyone," Ms. Andre called. "Today we're going to begin our discussion of gender differences and how society views those differences."

The boys let out a groan. The girls glanced around at each other, wondering what that meant exactly.

"First of all, does anyone know what gender means?" Ms. Andre asked.

Emma raised her hand. Tom crumpled up a piece of paper to throw at her, but Ms. Andre stared him down and he sank low in his seat.

"How about you, Brad?" Ms. Andre asked. "Do you have a gender?"

"Uh . . ." Brad looked embarrassed. "You mean like, in my pants?"

Everyone burst out laughing.

"No, gender means which sex you are," Ms. Andre explained. "You're a boy, I assume?"

"Oh. Yeah, I guess so," Brad said. Several girls pointed at him and giggled.

"Most living things have a gender," Ms. Andre said. "They are either male or female." While Ms. Andre wrote MALE and FEMALE on the board, Brad poked Tom and pointed at Kelly Angstrom. Talk about female! She was the most beautiful girl in sixth grade. She had silky strawberry blond hair, creamy skin, and some serious curves. Today she was wearing a red V-neck sweater. If you looked at her from the right angle, as Tom and Brad were now trying to do, you could sort of see her . . .

"Tom? How about you?" Ms. Andre asked suddenly.

"What?"

"What are some of the characteristics of your gender?"

"Uh . . . well, I'm a . . . boy." Tom's face turned red.

"That's right," Ms. Andre said. "So what are some of the characteristics of boys?"

"Uh . . . ," Tom mumbled. "They like sports?"

Ms. Andre wrote SPORTS on the board. "Are sports something that only boys like?"

"*No*," Emma said. "Girls like sports."

"Yeah," another girl added. "Who says girls don't like sports?"

"Well, they're not very good at them," Tom said

"Jane Hennessey whipped your butt this morning!" Courtney said.

"If it weren't for your stupid Grrlzillas, I would have gotten her out!"

Courtney snickered. "Whatever. You just wanted to look up Margaret's skirt!"

"That was a total accident!"

"Settle down, class," Ms. Andre said. "Could we say that society *assumes* that only boys like sports, but in reality, girls like sports too?"

"Who cares what girls like," Brad grumbled.

"All right, Brad," Ms. Andre said. "Good to know you're listening. What characteristics do girls have that boys don't?"

Brad thought about it. "Uh . . . they talk a lot?"

"Don't boys talk?"

"Not like girls," Brad said. "Girls blab their heads off. That's all they ever do. Blah, blah, blah, blah. They never shut up."

"At least we have something to say," Emma interjected.

"Yeah," Courtney said. "At least we have actual brains."

"Okay, okay, that's enough," Ms. Andre said. "I think everyone can agree that both boys and girls have actual brains. At least in theory." She looked around the class. "Margaret? Can you think of anything about boys that is a characteristic of their gender?"

Margaret couldn't think of an answer.

"Are boys' bodies different from girls'?" Ms. Andre went on.

"Yeah," cried Courtney. "They get boners when they slow-dance."

All the boys cracked up. Some of the girls did too. Emma could feel her cheeks turn bright red.

"Courtney is correct," Ms. Andre said. "Though let's try not to use the B word." She turned around and wrote ERECTION on the board instead.

Then Jeff Matthews raised his hand. "Yes, Jeff? Do you have something to add?" Ms. Andre asked.

Jeff smiled at Ms. Andre. "Yeah," he said, leaning back in his chair. "To me, it's more about the vibe. Boys, like, have a different groove than girls. Boys are more about chillin' with their Game Boys or shredding on their dirt bikes. Girls are more about hanging with their homegirls and watchin' the hotties on MTV."

All the girls swooned over Jeff's brilliance. Brad pounded his forehead on his desk.

"That's good, Jeff," Ms. Andre said. "You have some valid perceptions. Now, *understanding* gender differences— that's where it gets interesting. Which brings me to this week's assignment."

Tom could feel something bad coming, some touchy-feely assignment, and probably homework. He snuck another look at Kelly. Her sweater was revealing even more than before. If only he could . . . Tom looked down at his lap and tried to think of something else: baseball, dirt bikes, car crashes. If he didn't stop thinking about Kelly, he'd be stuck in his health classroom all day long.

EMMA LIKES JEFF!

As usual, it was raining when school let out. Emma waited for the bus under the big blue awning with Courtney. When it arrived, she and Courtney sat in the middle seats. Emma hoped they could talk more about Jeff Matthews, but of course, Courtney was too busy teasing Brad.

"Hey, Brad," Courtney said. "That was awesome in health class, when you figured out you're a boy. You're *sooo* smart."

"Look. Queen Kong speaks."

"Maybe by next year you'll figure out what a girl is."

"I already know what girls are." Brad kicked the bottom of their seat. "A big pile of crapola, served steaming hot on a plate!"

"Oh, Brad, I love it when you talk about your dining habits." Courtney made googly eyes at him. "Tell me more."

Emma hoped Courtney didn't expect her to say anything funny.

Brad and Courtney kept at each other until they reached Brad's stop. Soon after, Courtney was dropped off at her house and the bus grew quiet. Emma was stuck with Tom and the few other people who lived on Birch Street, the last stop on the bus.

Emma glanced at Tom. He had pulled something out of his pocket. It looked like a small arrowhead. Tom was always hanging out in the woods, exploring and looking for stuff. He used to ask her to go with him.

"What's that?" she asked.

"None of your business."

"I can ask you a question if I want," Emma said. Why did he have to be so rude? She looked at the arrowhead. "Where'd you get it?"

"Nowhere."

She sighed. "I can see it's an arrowhead. I was just wondering where you got it."

"That's for me to know—"

"And for me to find out. Jeez, you're so original." Emma glared at him. "By the way, the stuff you said in health class was pure genius too. Girls don't like sports? That's ridiculous."

"They might like 'em," Tom said confidently. "They just can't play 'em."

"That's so not true."

"It is," Tom said. "It's a proven fact."

"Proven by who?"

Tom slipped the arrowhead back in his pocket. "By everyone. Girls aren't as good at football or baseball. Or tennis. Or golf."

"How about gymnastics?"

"Maybe at gymnastics." Tom shrugged. "But gymnastics isn't a real sport."

"*What?*" Emma couldn't believe this.

"Oh, c'mon. Rolling around on the floor? Swinging on bars?"

"Excuse me? Have you ever watched the Olympics? Not only is it a *real* sport, gymnastics is one of the *oldest* sports in the world."

"It might be old. But it's not baseball."

"Baseball? What's baseball? A bunch of fat guys hitting a ball with a stick."

"Real sports have teams," Tom explained slowly. "That's why they call it *team sports.*"

"That is so stupid." Emma turned away and stared out the window at the passing houses and the green lawns. Just then they went by Jeff Matthews's house. He was in the driveway, helping his mom unload groceries from their minivan.

"Oh my God!" Emma pressed her face against the glass.

Tom tried to follow her gaze. "What are you looking at?"

"Nothing," Emma said, sitting back in her seat. But it was too late.

"Well, it's Pretty Boy Matthews!" he said. "Mr. Playah himself."

"He is not a *player*," Emma said.

"Are you kidding? That guy had four girlfriends last summer."

"He happens to be very nice. Which is something girls appreciate."

"Do *you* like him?"

"No," Emma said quickly, hoping her cheeks didn't betray her. "Of course not. I mean . . . well . . . he's definitely one of the cuter—"

"You *do* like him!" Tom bounced on his seat. "You like Jeff Matthews!"

"I do not! I never said that!"

"Emma likes Jeff, Emma likes Jeff!" teased Tom. "Does the playah know about this?"

"No, he doesn't, and you better not say anything! If you do, I swear I'll—"

"You'll what? Tell the Grrlzillas?" Tom laughed. "You are so busted."

"You can't tell," pleaded Emma. "Please. C'mon, Tom, you can't."

Tom sat back with a huge grin on his face.

Emma crossed her arms angrily over her chest and stared out the window, seeing nothing. She had never thought she could dislike Tom, but she had been absolutely, positively one hundred percent wrong.

She hated him.

A BOY'S LIFE

At home, Tom yelled hi to his mom in the kitchen and ran up the stairs to his room. His walls and desk were covered with baseball posters, programs, and statistics printouts. Since the Seattle Mariners were his favorite team, he had a Mariners wastebasket, a Mariners bedspread—even a Mariners mouse pad.

He went online and checked the Mariners score. Sometimes when the Ms played on the East Coast, the games were over by the time he got home from school. Today the Ms had beaten the dreaded Yankees, which was always good news. It would have been even better if his dad had been around to gloat with him about the victory. But his mom and dad had gotten a divorce two years before, and his father had moved to an apartment downtown. It still felt weird. Tom missed seeing his dad read the box scores at the kitchen table during breakfast and hearing him say, "Good night, champ," before Tom went to sleep.

Before Tom could dwell on it too much, he grabbed his glove and ran downstairs to practice pitching against the fence in the backyard. He had drawn a chalk strike zone on the wooden planks and built a pitcher's mound with dirt from his mom's garden. But he couldn't find his plastic bucket of old baseballs. He usually kept it on top of the sports cabinet in the garage so that his little brother couldn't reach it. But it wasn't there anymore. That was odd. Maybe he'd left them somewhere else and forgotten.

He went inside. "Mom!" he yelled. "Have you seen my baseballs?"

Then his little brother ran through the house. Ricky Witherspoon was a ferocious, black-haired seven-year-old. He was with his friend William, their neighbor from across the street. The two of them hacked at each other with plastic light sabers. They crashed through the room like they always did, knocking things over left and right. Ricky really got on Tom's nerves, especially when important things like his baseballs were missing.

"Hey! Ricky!" Tom said loudly.

Ricky didn't answer. He almost broke a lamp as he swung wildly at William.

"*Hey!*" Tom caught the light saber with his hand and jerked it away from Ricky. "Where are my baseballs?"

"What?"

"My baseballs. I had a bucket of them on top of the sports cabinet. Where are they?"

"I don't know." Ricky grabbed for his weapon. "Gimme my light saber back."

"Not until I get my baseballs back."

"You mean the hand grenades?" William asked.

"What hand grenades?" Tom said. "Did you use them as hand grenades?"

A very guilty look spread across Ricky's face.

Tom sighed. "Show me where they are."

The three of them walked down the street to the creek. William pointed to the big drainage pipe where the creek ran under Birch Street.

"You threw my baseballs into that pipe?" Tom asked.

William nodded. "Ricky said we had to blow it up," he said. "Or the water ninjas would get us."

One look from Tom and Ricky bolted toward the house. As usual, Ricky ran straight to their mother. She always favored Ricky because he was smaller and younger than Tom. But did that make it okay for him to be a baseball-stealing maniac? Tom didn't think so.

"Calm down," said his mother. "Both of you. We'll get some new ones next time we're at the mall." This was the same thing she had said when Ricky popped Tom's bike tires, broke Tom's pocketknife, and packed Tom's football helmet full of mud.

"But what do I do until then?" Tom protested. "Tryouts are on Thursday. I have to practice."

"Call one of your friends," his mother replied. "I'm sure they'll let you borrow a baseball."

I should call my dad, Tom thought. But he didn't say it. Instead, he got his glove and rode his bike to Brad's house.

A
GIRL'S
LIFE

When Emma got home, she was too upset to say hi to her mother. She went straight to her room and threw herself on her bed. What would she do if Tom told everyone she liked Jeff? What if the whole school found out? She picked up her phone and speed-dialed Courtney. She would know what to do. It wasn't like Tom didn't have his own crushes. Every girl in sixth grade knew he stared at Kelly Angstrom every chance he got. If he dared to say anything, Emma would go right up to Kelly and . . .

She gazed around her room while the phone rang. It was pretty lame by sixth-grade standards. She didn't have anything fun on her walls, except for a dorky picture of Hilary Duff and an old *School of Rock* poster. This was partly her mom's fault. When she wasn't scheduling new activities for Emma, Mrs. Baker was closely monitoring Emma's walls, notebooks, and desk area for any "inappropriate images." She did not approve of girls' covering their room with pictures of "half-naked boys."

No one was home at Courtney's. Emma hung up and clutched the phone to her chest. Should she call Tom? Try to reason with him? It was so strange how different he had become. But then, a lot of guys were acting weird lately. Teasing girls for no reason. Doing weird, pervy things. And next year was seventh grade. It was only going to get worse.

There was a loud knock on Emma's door. "Emma, do you have my Good Charlotte CD?"

It was her older sister, Claire. She and Emma had actually been close when they were younger. But now Claire was a freshman in high school, where she had suddenly become extremely "tight." She wore only "tight" clothes (Hot Topic, Goth House). She listened to "tight" bands (Good Charlotte, My Chemical Romance). And she only hung out with "tight" guys. (Claire never said who they were. Emma figured they were probably too "tight" to have names.)

The worst part? Not only was Claire committed to her own tightness, but she never missed a chance to point out how *untight* Emma was.

Emma stared at the door. "No."

"Yes, you do," said Claire. "It's not in my CD player and it's not downstairs. So you must have it."

Emma scanned the room. She had a stack of CDs and DVDs on her desk that her mom had dumped there. But before she could look through them, her sister barged in.

"Claire!" Emma hated when she did that. "Did I say you could come in?"

Claire pointed at Emma's desk. "See? There it is. I knew you had it." Claire went to Emma's desk and pulled a CD out of the pile. "I wonder what else of mine you have."

"I don't have anything of yours," Emma protested. "And I would never listen to Good Charlotte."

"Of course you wouldn't. That's why no boys like you."

"I don't care. I hate boys."

Claire raised an eyebrow at her sister. "Sounds like someone is having a little trouble with the opposite sex," she said. "But then, if you're still wearing jeans and pink hoodies, what do you expect? Even lame guys are sick of pink hoodies."

When she was gone, Emma flopped back on her bed, covering her face with her hands. Maybe Claire was right. Maybe she did need to update her look, her whole self, even. How else was she ever going to get Jeff to notice her? While other girls were becoming actual teenagers, she was becoming a straight-A activities dork.

Still, that was nothing compared to the embarrassment awaiting her if Tom started telling everyone about her crush on Jeff Matthews. . . .

AN UNUSUAL ASSIGNMENT

Wednesday morning, Tom strolled into health class and took his seat. He saw Emma staring at him from across the room. Actually, she'd stared at him during the whole bus ride to school too, and she hadn't said a word. She was obviously nervous that he would tell people about her crush.

But Tom hadn't told anyone—he'd barely thought about it. He had more important things to worry about, like lost baseballs, the upcoming Little League tryouts, and Kelly Angstrom, who was busy erasing the chalkboard. Today her jeans were so low you could see her underwear. Was that a thong?

"Okay, Kelly, that's enough," said Ms. Andre. Every boy watched Kelly walk back to her seat. "Now, as we discussed yesterday, our subject is gender differences. . . ."

People had thought this was funny the day before. They

were less amused now. Margaret began chewing on her pen. Kelly and Sienna passed lip gloss back and forth. A couple of guys began comparing playlists. Brad drew a picture of a gorilla wearing a diaper. He wrote *Courtney, Queen of the Grrlzillas* under it in flowing script.

Ms. Andre continued to talk. "For this assignment we will divide into boy/girl pairs. . . ."

People were barely listening, but when they heard the word "pairs," everyone sat up.

"I want each of you to stay in constant contact with your partner and observe every aspect of his or her life."

Tom shifted awkwardly in his chair. This did not sound good. The girls looked around in excited surprise. Boys? Pairs? Girls and boys in constant contact?

"I can't do this assignment," Brad said from the back of the room.

"Why not?" asked Ms. Andre.

"I have a medical condition," he said. "I'm allergic to girls." Everyone laughed.

"That's very funny, Brad. Maybe with your partner, *Margaret Cooper*, you can discuss why boys like to show off and tell jokes."

Brad's mouth dropped open in horror.

"Uh, Ms. Andre?" Margaret raised her hand. "I think I'm going to be sick. Can I go home, please?"

"No, Margaret. I know it sounds difficult, but you and Brad will be a good team."

Margaret Cooper stared at Brad. Then she dropped her head and began muttering to herself.

Ms. Andre handed out the assignment sheets. Tom took his and read:

HEALTH CLASS ASSIGNMENT
DUE MONDAY, MAY 15
ONE-PAGE ESSAY:
"GENDER DIFFERENCES"

Spend at least fifteen minutes every day talking to or meeting with your partner and discussing your day-to-day life, with special attention to how our gender creates differences in our lives.

1) When possible, try to think about how society assumes there are certain differences and how we play into those (or don't).

2) Think about how certain words and language create differences in how we see boys and girls. (For example: Boys who take control of an activity might be called leaders, while girls who do the same thing might be called bossy.)

The directions went on and on.

"I have to do this with Margaret?" Brad groaned.

Margaret scowled back. "Likewise."

"Now, the other pairs will be . . ." Ms. Andre began reading her list. The class listened anxiously as each pair was read.

"Craig Foltz will be with Sienna Jones. Rick Malin will be with Courtney Hall. . . ."

Tom folded his hands beneath his desk and prayed for Kelly Angstrom. That would be the break of a lifetime, perhaps even better than making the junior Little League team! He looked around the room and caught Emma staring at Jeff. *Big surprise.*

Finally, Tom heard his own name. "Tom Witherspoon will be with . . ."

Tom's hands went cold. His heart began to pound. *Kelly Angstrom, Kelly Angstrom . . .*

"Emma Baker."

"What?" said Tom. "But—"

"No!" Emma said. "Ms. Andre! You don't understand!"

Ms. Andre stopped reading from her list. "What don't I understand?"

"We can't be together," Tom said.

"Why is that?"

"Because we . . . we're neighbors," Emma said. "We already know each other."

"So?"

"So isn't the point to learn about someone we don't know?" Emma asked.

Ms. Andre gave them both a sly look. "Since you know each other so well, your papers will be especially good, won't they?" She went back to reading her list.

"Way to go," Tom called out to Emma. "Now look what you did!"

Emma scowled at him. "It's not my fault!"

"Yes it is!"

Emma raised her hand again. "Ms. Andre? Is this paper going to count toward our grade?"

"Yes, Emma. This paper will count as half of your grade for this section of class."

"What about the other half?" Ashley asked.

"Your partner's grade will be the other half."

"But Ms. Andre!" moaned a half-dozen girls around the room.

"Look at that," Ms. Andre said. "Only the girls are complaining. Could that be a gender difference? Is everyone taking notes? Obviously this exercise will be good for all of you."

"Good for us like green vegetables?" grumbled Brad. "Or like flu shots?"

"Like both," said Ms. Andre. "Now get to work."

EMMA CONFRONTS TOM

Emma, who had gotten straight As all year, immediately began to worry about the gender assignment. She went looking for Tom during lunch. He was sitting with the other sixth-grade boys in a far corner of the cafeteria. As usual, the boys' table was littered with half-eaten rolls, vegetables that had been flung around, and crushed milk cartons. Zach Leland was busy smushing potatoes, Jell-O, and ketchup together in his fruit cup. Emma tried to hide her disgust.

"Tom, can I talk to you?"

"What about?" Tom asked.

"Our report."

Tom was too busy dissecting his hot dog to get up. "What about it? We'll work on it in class."

"Can you just come here a minute?"

Looking totally put out, Tom reluctantly stood and came around the table.

"In case you haven't noticed, I'm a good student," Emma told him. "And I know you are . . . well, slightly challenged in that area. So if you wouldn't mind, I'd like to do a good job on these essays so we can both get a good grade."

"That sounds great," Tom said. "Why don't you work really hard and get us an A. I never get As, so I'm curious about what that's like."

Emma forced a smile. "Tom, you don't understand. If you don't help, neither of us will get an A or even a B."

"Fine, but we'll work on it in class. Because I don't do homework. I don't believe in it. Besides, I have other things to do, important things—"

"Like trying to see down Kelly Angstrom's shirt?"

"Hey, I never—"

"Do you even realize how obvious you are?" Emma sighed. Boys were so transparent. "How obvious *all* boys are?"

"Well, why don't you write that down and get us a good grade, because I'm not doing any extra work." Tom popped a large piece of hot dog into his mouth. "It would be worth getting a D, just to watch you freak out."

"I am *not* getting a D," Emma said sternly.

"Do whatever you want. I have baseball tryouts tomorrow, so if you want me, you know where I'll be. On the baseball field. Practicing."

Emma glared at him. "Why are you being like this? Why are you always so impossible?"

"I'm impossible? You're the one who's impossible!"

"I'm just doing what we're supposed to do!"

"That's another difference between boys and girls," Tom said. "Girls always try to be Little Miss Do-Right. Well, guess what? I do what I want. Ms. Andre can give me a D for all I care."

Just then a gob of mashed potatoes flew between them. Brad had flicked it with his spoon. He laughed at the two of them. "Jeez, you guys. At least you don't have Margaret Cooper as your partner."

It was pointless to even attempt to have a mature conversation. Emma turned on her heel and marched away.

"Hey, you should try getting a D sometime," Tom yelled after her. "It's fun. Once you get a D, there's nowhere to go but up!"

Emma spent the rest of the day stewing. Why had Ms. Andre done this to her? After last period, Emma went to her locker and loaded up her backpack. She had gymnastics right after school.

Gymnastics was Emma's favorite time of the day. They had great equipment at George Wilson. There were brand-new floor mats and mirrors along two walls. They had the good chalk Emma liked to coat her hands with between routines. And she liked the coach, Mrs. Weissman, who always came up with fun choreography for the girls to do during their floor exercises.

A couple of girls were already stretching when Emma went in. Emma stretched too, and then ran through the first part of her floor routine. However, she couldn't get Tom out of her mind. The idea of working with him on a school project—*any* school project—was basically her worst nightmare. She had other worries as well: a piano lesson that afternoon, an extra-credit social studies report, a Girl Scout cookie sale the next day. Plus, her mom had volunteered her for two nights at the senior center the following week. Not to mention the biggest thing of all—the gymnastics meet on Saturday. How would she have time to make Tom do the project with her?

These thoughts were ruining her workout. At one point, she slipped doing a forward handspring and landed flat on her back. She winced from the pain.

"Emma, you're not concentrating," Mrs. Weissman said. "What are you thinking about?"

Emma stared up from the floor. "Trust me. You don't have time to hear it all."

"Well, whatever it is, it's hurting your workout. You're going to injure yourself. Why don't you go upstairs and work on the trampoline. See if you can get your rhythm back."

Emma picked up her towel and did as she was told. Then she thought of Tom calling her Little Miss Do-Right. It was true. Emma did what everyone else wanted her to. She tried to remember the last time she had done something on her own, but she couldn't. For a minute, she felt jealous of Tom. He always did what he wanted, and somehow he got away with it. Boys really were different. They seemed to feel no responsibility to anyone but themselves.

TOM GETS
A LITTLE
TRAMPOLINE
ACTION

Tom sat underneath the awning in front of school, waiting for his father to pick him up. His dad had played baseball in college and was Tom's best hope for some last-minute coaching before the tryouts. As usual, he was late. Tom understood that his dad often got stuck in meetings. But it was hard not to get upset when his father didn't come through for him.

Tom's cell phone rang. His dad's number flashed across the screen.

"I'm sorry, Tom." His dad sounded frenzied. "I'm absolutely swamped, and I have clients coming in on short notice to look at plans. There's no way I can make it."

"But tryouts are tomorrow," Tom pleaded. "And Ricky lost all my practice balls."

"He lost them all? He lost *twenty* baseballs?"

"He and William threw them down the drainage pipe."

"Hmm, well, I'll get you some more. I'll FedEx them. Don't worry, champ. Things will work out."

"Yeah," Tom said. "They'll work out like last year. I'll be on the B team with all the wussy guys."

"Hey, don't talk like that. You had a very respectable season last year, and I want you to—" There was silence, then muffled talking. "Tom, my clients just arrived. I have to go."

Tom clicked off and slumped back on the bench. Disappointed once again. Now there would be no practice, and he didn't even have a ride home because he'd missed the last bus.

He walked to the playground to see if he could find people for a pickup game, but the baseball diamond was deserted. He wandered back to the main gym and stuck his head in the door. The trampoline was set up and the gym was empty. Tom loved the trampoline. They'd had it in gym class that week, but Mrs. Weissman hadn't let them do anything fun. Maybe he could sneak a little tramp action. He checked outside to make sure no one was around. Then he slipped quietly inside.

The gym seemed bigger when there were no kids in it. Tom could hear his footsteps echoing as he approached the trampoline. He hit the rubbery surface with his fist and felt his hand bounce off. He looked around one last time to make sure he was alone. Then he kicked off his shoes and crawled on.

Tom moved to the middle, steadied himself, and then remembered the very sharp arrowhead he still had in his hip pocket. He moved it to the ankle pocket of his cargo pants so he wouldn't stab himself.

Then he began to bounce. Should he try a flip? He could do them on a diving board, and Jeff Matthews had done one during gym when Mrs. Weissman wasn't looking. Naturally all the girls had seen it. If Jeff could do one, they couldn't be *that* hard. Tom thought about Emma. She could probably do one. She could do anything. Tom felt a little jealous of her and her endless activities. At least Emma was good at stuff and achieving things.

Suddenly, as if he'd summoned her somehow, Emma Baker appeared next to the trampoline. She was in her gymnastics leotard and she didn't look happy to see him.

"Uh, excuse me?" she said. "Are you on the gymnastics team?"

Tom kept bouncing. "No."

"Then why are you on *our* trampoline?"

"Because I feel like it."

"You know people are not allowed on the trampoline without permission. Mrs. Weissman will *freak* if she sees you here."

"So?" said Tom.

"So, I'm supposed to be on it. Mrs. Weissman sent me here."

"So? There's room for two."

There *was* room for two. It was a big trampoline. Emma stared at Tom for a moment, then sighed. "All right," she said, kicking off her ballet flats. "But you better not get me in trouble. . . ."

She climbed on and began to bounce. Tom continued to bounce on his side. But with Emma bouncing beside him, the trampoline didn't respond the same way. Tom wasn't bouncing as high, and he was having trouble keeping his rhythm.

"When there's two people, you have to go together," said Emma.

"I don't want to go together."

"You *have* to go together, or we can't both be on it. If we don't bounce together, we'll fall off."

"Since when are you the boss of the trampoline?"

"I happen to be a gymnast," Emma said in that superior way she had lately. "I happen to know what I'm talking about."

"Well, I *happen* to not care," said Tom.

But Emma was right. Not bouncing together was throwing him off. He lost his balance. He almost fell over the side. Then he nearly hit Emma.

"Stay on your side!" Emma scolded, her hair flopping up.

"I'm trying to. Don't push me!"

"I'm *not* pushing you."

"Yes, you are. And I was here first."

"You're not even supposed to be on here!"

Tom tried to get his rhythm back, but he was all over the place. On his next bounce, he nearly collided with Emma.

"Watch out!" she cried.

"I'm trying to! It's just hard 'cause you're so small!"

He bounced far away from her, but that just sent him springing back into the center. He was totally off balance now, and he was on a collision course with Emma. He could see her head coming right at his. He couldn't stop, he couldn't control himself, he couldn't—

Thock!

Their heads collided like billiard balls. A bright red flash exploded in Tom's eyes. For a moment, he felt his brain floating, his body floating, everything drifting serenely in space.

And then everything went black.

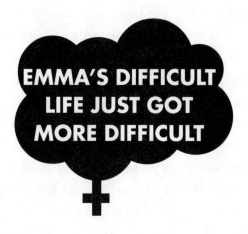

EMMA'S DIFFICULT LIFE JUST GOT MORE DIFFICULT

Emma had been knocked out, or something. She wasn't sure what had happened. She lifted her head and found herself hanging off the side of the trampoline. She rolled over and dropped to the floor. Her head hurt terribly. She didn't feel like herself.

She heard the locker-room door slam. She looked around. Where was Tom? She felt dizzy and strange on her feet. She'd heard about concussions from gymnastics coaches. People hit their heads and were confused for hours. Sometimes they couldn't remember their own phone numbers.

Then she heard a scream. It was a girl's scream, coming from the boys' locker room. That was odd. What was a girl doing in there? It was probably another Brad Hailey prank. He had probably tricked Margaret into some embarrassing situation. Emma couldn't let that happen. She *was* a

Grrlzilla, after all. She lurched along on wobbly feet to the boys' locker room and yanked open the door.

Emma had never been in a boys' locker room before. The air was thick and musky. A waist-high wire basket full of smelly gym towels leaned against the door. She cautiously ventured forward. She was no doubt breaking several rules by being there.

She turned to her left, toward the sink and the showers. She expected to see a gang of laughing boys and poor Margaret wearing a jockstrap on her head. What she found was one girl, dressed in a gymnastics leotard and tights identical to her own, standing at the mirror grabbing at her arms and chest and completely freaking out. From the back, the girl looked vaguely familiar. When the girl turned around, Emma gasped. The girl was . . . her.

"What the—" Emma murmured.

"It's you!" screamed the girl, who looked exactly like Emma. "And you look like me! What are you doing in my clothes?"

Emma looked down at herself. It was true. She was dressed in strange clothes. Actually, they were *Tom's* clothes. But how could that be?

She looked at the girl. "And that's you? Tom? In my—"

"Yes, yes, it's me. And I look like you!"

"And I'm a . . . ," Emma said, still inspecting her arms and legs. "Oh my God, we've switched clothes!"

"Not just our clothes!" Tom said through her mouth, with her voice. He shoved her in front of the mirror. What she saw was more horrifying than any scary movie. Tom's wiry hair. His freckled nose. A crust of ketchup on his chin. She reached up to swipe it off and felt her own skin under her fingers. She was . . . Tom!

Beside her, Tom began to hyperventilate. "I've got your hair! I've got your—" He began to touch parts of himself. He touched his face, his chest, and then lightly patted the front of his shorts. "Oh *no!*" he shrieked. "It's gone!"

Emma stared at her fingers and hands. Her forearms were thicker. Her chest felt heavier. It was like she had turned into the Hulk.

"This can't be!" she said, panic rising in her voice—no, *Tom's* voice. "What happened?"

They both touched themselves, shocked by what they found, or *didn't* find.

Tom grabbed Emma. "Listen, this isn't funny. You gotta give me my body back."

"You give me *my* body back!" Emma said. "I didn't do this, you did it!"

"How did I do it? Don't blame me!"

"Wait, wait, wait. Okay. I know what this is. This is a *hallucination*. We hit our heads. We're unconscious. And now we're having a dream."

"Both of us?"

"It's possible." Emma reached for Tom and took his girl hands in hers. "So now if we just calm down and close our eyes, in a second we'll wake up."

"Okay," Tom said.

They both stood still and closed their eyes, but when they opened them, nothing had happened.

"I'm not turning back!" said Tom, a new panic in his voice.

"I'm not either!"

"Maybe if we hit our heads again," Tom suggested. "Maybe if we go back to the trampoline."

"But someone might come."

"So we'll do it here. We'll run into each other."

"Okay," Emma said, desperate.

They backed away from each other. The locker room was quiet and bright around them. They stared into each other's eyes. They both set their feet and braced for impact.

"You go first," Emma said.

"No, you go."

"Why do I have to go?"

"Just go!"

"Fine," Emma said. She gritted her teeth and prepared to run into her old body, but then she stopped. "Shouldn't we have safety helmets or something?"

"Safety helmets?" Tom cried. "Would you run into me, please?"

"But it's gonna hurt. And I already have a headache."

"So do I," Tom said. He looked around the gym. "I know. We'll wrap towels around our heads!" He ran to the stinky towel basket and began wrapping his head with one.

Emma did the same. But the towel she picked up smelled like dirty underwear. "This towel is disgusting!"

"Get another one!"

Emma grabbed a second towel and held it as far from her nose as she could. She wrapped it around her head.

"Now run into me!" Tom had his eyes squeezed closed.

"I can't. I don't know how," said Emma. "You're the boy. You run into me."

"Dude, hello? I'm not the boy anymore. You're the boy."

"But I'm not a *real* boy," Emma wailed, on the verge of tears.

"You look pretty real to me!"

"Fine. Get ready." Emma prepared to crash into Tom. Then she stopped. "I can't. You're a girl. That's not fair."

"But I'm not really a girl. You just said that!"

"This is too confusing," said Emma. "Here, maybe I can do it this way." She stood closer to Tom and gripped his ears.

Tom had a worried look on his face. "What are you doing?"

"Don't worry, it won't hurt." Emma took a deep breath, held his ears, and banged her forehead into his. But she was much stronger now than she realized, and what she meant to be a gentle bump sent Tom sprawling onto the floor.

"Owwww!" Tom winced and held his forehead. "What are you doing?"

"Trying to knock heads!"

"Well, you don't have to knock me out!"

Emma looked at Tom writhing around on the floor. "This is really happening," she murmured. "I'm too strong for my own good. I'm acting like a complete idiot. And I smell like somebody's crotch. Oh my God, I'm totally a *boy*!"

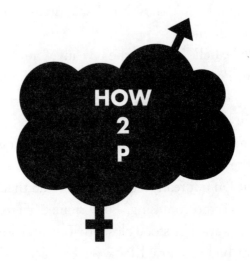

HOW
2
P

Suddenly, male voices rang out from outside the locker room. There were boys in the gym, and they were coming toward the door.

"Who is that?" cried Emma.

"It must be the track team."

"What do we do?"

"Follow me." Tom clutched Emma's thick wrist and led her through the locker room to the janitor's closet. Guys sometimes hid from the gym teacher there, or locked up fifth graders. Tom and Emma jammed themselves inside and Tom pulled the door closed, which was not easy with Emma's tiny arms.

In the darkness, they knocked into mops and squirt bottles. Emma fumbled around and stepped into a bucket. She couldn't get her foot out. "What's wrong with your feet?" she whispered.

"Nothing."

"They're huge!"

"Be quiet!"

"I feel like Frankenstein or something."

"Would you shut up?"

Now the locker room filled with boys, laughing, teasing, and bragging about the track meet. Tom could hear the showers turn on. Two boys walked by the door, inches from where they were hiding.

"How long will they be out there?" Emma whispered. "I have to go. I have a piano lesson at four."

"You can't go to a piano lesson," Tom said. "You're me!"

"Then I have to call and cancel. Or she charges you for the lesson."

"Shhhh!" Tom whispered. "We have a lot bigger problems than your stupid piano lesson!"

Emma tried to get her foot out of the bucket. Tom grabbed it but didn't have the strength to yank it off. He was a girl. He had no muscle. He had no pitching arm! He had no . . . *gender* in his pants! This was pure insanity.

"We have to figure out what happened to us," Tom whispered. "Think about what we did. What could have caused this?"

"It's obvious what caused it," Emma whispered. "*You* got on the trampoline."

"So?"

"So, students aren't supposed to go on the trampoline unsupervised."

Tom shook his head in frustration. "You think *that's*

why we're in different bodies? Because we broke some stupid rule?"

"I don't know," Emma said. "But I didn't do anything wrong. It's not my fault. I don't want to be a boy."

Tom said nothing. Then he thought he heard her sniffling. This was completely unacceptable. "Are you crying? Oh my God, you're *not* crying."

"I can't help it," Emma whimpered. "This is stressful."

"You have to help it. You're me now! I don't cry. I'm a baseball player. I'm a pitcher!"

Emma managed to stop crying. Then, by twisting her foot a certain way, she got it out of the bucket. But then she stepped on a scrub brush and fell into Tom. This was getting ridiculous. Every time she turned or shifted she knocked into something.

"Okay, listen," Tom whispered. "If we don't switch back in the next couple minutes, we'll just have to fake it until we do. We'll pretend to be each other. And by that I mean we will try not to act like deranged farm animals, okay?"

"That's easy for you to say," protested Emma. "You got smaller."

"And then," Tom continued, "we'll think about this logically and we'll switch back."

"But how long is that going to take?"

"How would I know?"

Just then two boys walked by the janitor's door. "Did you see me torch that guy in the hundred-meter?" said one.

"What a butt-nugget!" said the other.

"And did you see their guy with the javelin?"

"That dude threw like a girl!"

Tom didn't like the sound of that. He looked down at his hands. They were small, delicate girl hands. He didn't want to be a girl. He wanted to be *torching* someone at something. He wanted to be a boy.

The two voices went away. Tom and Emma stood and waited. Several minutes went by. Neither of them said a word.

"So if I'm supposed to be a guy," Emma finally whispered, "I just have one question."

"What?"

"How do you . . ."

"How do you what?"

"How do boys, you know, how do they . . . go to the bathroom?"

"Are you serious?" Tom groaned.

"Well, how would I know? I don't have any brothers."

"You just do it. You just go."

"But like, how do you do it . . . standing up?"

Tom tried to see her face in the dark. He couldn't, which was probably just as well. "You just hold it in your hand."

"And that's it?"

"You aim it. You know, so you don't get any on your shoes or whatever."

"Oh, gross!"

"Well, you asked." Tom grunted. He thought for a moment. "Actually, there's one more thing."

"What?"

Tom couldn't believe he was talking about this, but he had no choice. What if Emma got caught walking around with pee on her pants, on *his* pants? "At the end, after you're done, you kind of wiggle it."

"You wiggle it?"

"You just kind of shake it once or twice. It's no big deal, all guys do it."

"Oh, right," said Emma. "Ms. Andre showed us a film about that. Masturbation."

"No! Not *masturbation*!" said Tom. "That's totally different! This is just for going to the bathroom. You shake it a little before you zip up to make sure you're done. Jeez!"

"Okay, okay," Emma said. "Don't have a conniption."

Tom put his ear to the door and tried to listen. All he could hear were the showers. "Since we're talking about it," he whispered. "How do girls do it?"

"You sit."

"I know *that*. But then what do you do?"

"And then you go."

"And it goes where you want it to?" he asked.

"Hopefully," Emma said. "And then you use toilet paper."

Tom got down on his knees to try to see under the door. "Yeah, that's why my mom always runs out."

"But wait," said Emma, watching him. "If we're going to be each other, then you have to go to my piano lesson."

"I'm not going to any piano lesson." Tom stood up and dusted his hands off.

"You should also avoid covering yourself with dirt. Girls are clean."

"If I can't get dirty, then you can't cry."

"I'll cry if I have to cry. This isn't exactly easy, you know."

48

Despite himself, Tom felt sorry for her. Usually, Emma was so together and strong. Now, in his body, she seemed fragile.

But just then, there was a new noise outside their door. "Did you hear that?" asked a male voice.

"Is someone in the janitor's closet?" said another.

"Check it out. Someone's in there!"

Tom heard footsteps approaching. An expert at sneaking and hiding, he jumped away from the door and pressed himself against the wall. He was amazed at how little he was and what a tiny space he could fit himself into.

Emma, being a clueless girl, had no idea what to do. She'd never hidden from anyone in her life. When the door opened, she stood helplessly in the light.

BUSTED!

When the janitor's-closet door opened, Emma found herself face to face with two half-naked eighth-grade boys. They were both dripping wet and had towels wrapped around their waists. Should she scream? Run? She froze.

Before she could do anything, the boys laughed.

"Check it out, it's a sixth grader," said the taller one. He laughed.

"It's that Tom guy, the kid who thinks he can pitch," said the other.

"Tom! Dawg! What are you doing here?"

"You're me," whispered the real Tom from his hiding place. He tilted his chin at Emma to talk.

"Oh," Emma mumbled, turning back to face them. "Hey, guys." She tried to shrug in a boylike way. "What's up . . . dogs?"

The boys watched her with amusement. Swirls of steam billowed from the showers behind them. "That's kind of what we were wondering. Like, why are you in that closet?"

"I was just . . . uhhhhh . . ." Emma's nervous grin began to fade. What was she doing here? "I was just looking for some . . . cleaning stuff?"

The boys, who had seemed to expect some prank, or something funny going on, now began to frown. "Cleaning stuff?" the tall one repeated.

"I mean . . . I was . . . I thought maybe . . ."

"You're not hiding from someone?" said the other boy. "You're just hanging out in the janitor's closet?"

"Dude, that's a little *weird*," said the tall one.

Emma knew she was not handling this well. She was about to make Tom the laughingstock of the school. She tried to think of something cool to say, but all of a sudden Tom stepped beside her.

The boys both grabbed for their towels. "Whoooaa, dude!" one of the guys said.

"Girl in the room!" yelled someone else.

Tom dashed through the locker room, escaping easily out the front door.

The guys turned back to Emma. Now they were smiling from ear to ear. "Dawg! You had a chick in there!"

"Check it out!" they called to the other guys. "Tom Witherspoon had a girl in the janitor's closet!"

Emma blushed, and since she could think of no better way to react, she began nodding her oversized head in affirmation.

51

"Awesome!" cried an eighth grader.

"Score!"

"You get 'em, dawg!"

More of them gathered around. "And that was not just any sixth-grade girl, that was Straight-A Emma Baker!" Bryce Andrews, captain of the track team, looked impressed. "How'd you get *her* to make out with you?"

"Things are changing for our little Tommy," said a different boy, pushing Bryce away. "He's obviously got the moves."

"You old dawg, you!"

"Go get 'em, playah!"

With that, Emma was led out of the locker room as if she had won the big game. She was congratulated, saluted, and referred to as "dawg" about ten more times.

"See you later . . . dogs," she told them when they let her out of the gym. She was a little sorry to have to go. It was fun to have eighth graders congratulating you. For anything.

Tom was waiting for her outside the gym. "What on earth were you doing?" he demanded.

"What do you mean?"

"In the closet! If I hadn't run out of there, they'd have thought the *real* Tom Witherspoon was some sort of freak. Hanging out in the janitor's closet? Do you know how much of a loser that would make me?"

"Yeah, but now they all think I was in there with you!" Emma said. The negative implications of this were now dawning on her. "Now I'm going to get a reputation. People are going to think I'm some sort of wild girl."

"So what? That's a lot better than being a loser."

"Are you crazy?" Emma crossed her meaty arms. "Being a wild girl is way worse than being a loser!"

"What do you mean? People like wild girls," Tom said. "Nobody likes a loser."

"Yeah?" Emma said. "Who likes wild girls?"

"Lots of people. Boys."

"That's ridiculous!" Emma said. The two of them walked to the front of the school. "And not only will they think I make out with boys, they'll think I made out with *you*!"

"At least they'll stop thinking you're some uptight priss."

"Well, I'm not!" Emma declared. "I got a B in math last year!"

Tom suddenly stopped dead and looked down at himself. "Whoa, what is this thing I'm wearing?"

"It's a leotard."

"*Why* am I wearing a *leotard*?"

"Because that's what I was wearing, you idiot."

"And what are these shoes?" Tom moaned. "They're pixie slippers! I'm walking around in public dressed like a frickin' ballerina! Get this off me. Get this off me now!" He tried to rip off the leotard.

Emma grabbed Tom's tiny gymnast's body and shook him.

"Stop it! Calm down! Just go change into my school clothes." She found a piece of paper in Tom's coat and wrote down her locker combination. "It's locker ten."

"But what are your normal clothes going to be?" Tom looked like one of those cartoon characters with steam blowing out of its head. "I am not wearing a skirt. Or a bra!"

"Don't worry," Emma said. "I've got jeans and a T-shirt." She swallowed. "And you can just, uh, forget the bra."

"I swear to God. If *anyone* finds out . . ."

"Nobody's going to find out," Emma said. "We'll just do what you said. We'll fake it for a few hours until we can switch back. Now go change!"

Tom, who was looking more dazed and confused by the second, took the piece of paper and hurried into the girls' locker room. Emma sighed heavily as he walked away.

Then she turned and stared into the parking lot. There had to be an explanation for this. She'd figure it out and switch them back and life would go on. Eventually, she'd look back on this and think of it as a weird nightmare she'd once had. She slipped her hands in Tom's pockets as she thought about it and realized they were loaded with stuff. There were a shamrock key ring, a fake plastic eyeball, a broken skateboard wheel, a half-chewed bit of gum, three nickels, two pennies, and last but not least, a thick, gross, slimy tangle of month-old Gummi worms.

Emma stuffed them back in her pockets and wiped her hands on her cargo pants. Being a boy: It was not only several notches down on the intelligence scale, it was downright disgusting.

TOM'S FIRST PIANO LESSON

Emma's clothes were tiny. But so was Tom. He frantically dressed himself in the empty girls' locker room. The T-shirt Emma had mentioned was pink and had flowers all over it, and her jeans were embroidered! He didn't have time to groan about it, though, because as soon as he returned to the front of the school, Emma's mother arrived to take him to his piano lesson. Tom dragged Emma's very heavy book bag to the car and got in.

Mrs. Baker was a large, commanding woman with sharp, watchful eyes. "Are you okay?" she asked. "You look a little tired."

"I'm okay," Tom said cautiously. He didn't trust his voice.

Fortunately, Mrs. Baker's cell phone rang and she answered it. Tom sank down in the seat. He could barely see over the dashboard. Being Emma was like being six years old again.

As they drove through the suburbs, Tom remembered how strict Mrs. Baker was. She used to freak out over the tiniest thing, like if Tom rode his bike through her rose-bushes or accidentally hit a baseball through her kitchen window. Tom wasn't looking forward to spending the evening with someone *more* uptight than Emma.

After a few minutes, they arrived at a small brown house. Mrs. Baker parked in front and handed Tom a check. "Make sure you give this to Mrs. Rialto. It's for this month's piano lessons."

Tom took the check and jammed it into his pocket. Then Mrs. Baker leaned over to kiss Tom on the cheek, but he was so startled that he flinched and moved away.

Mrs. Baker gave him an odd look. "What's this? I can't give my own daughter a kiss good-bye anymore?"

Tom nervously shifted in his seat. "Um . . . I think I'm coming down with a cold. I don't want to get you sick."

"Well, I'll take the risk," Mrs. Baker said with a laugh, and kissed Tom. "Have a good lesson."

Tom hopped out of the car before any more awkward things could happen. He hurried up the cement walk, dragging Emma's huge backpack behind him. If only he could ditch it somehow. He felt so light and limber. He wanted to jump and run. Emma's body seemed capable of all sorts of things.

He knocked on Mrs. Rialto's door, but it was open, so he went in. The house had a waxy, Lysol smell to it. In the living room, a girl was hunched over the piano while Mrs. Rialto stood behind her. From the sound of things, the girl was messing up pretty badly.

"No! No!" Mrs. Rialto cried. "I want *lightness*! I want fingers prancing on air! *Caress* the keys!"

Oh brother, thought Tom. He made his way into the room beside the kitchen and took a seat. His lesson would start in five minutes. As he waited, panic began to set in. What was he going to do when it was his turn? He couldn't play the piano. He could barely play "Chopsticks."

He looked around the room. What could he do to get out of this? Earlier, Emma had told him to try to avoid Mrs. Rialto's dog, Millie, who sometimes nipped at the students. Right now, he could see that Millie was asleep under the kitchen table. But Tom also realized that Mrs. Rialto actually had a herd of pets. He spotted an enormous cat under a chair across the room. There was another cat in the middle of the floor, and a third sat on the windowsill. He had seen several birdcages in the front room by the piano too.

There was also some sewing stuff on the table beside him. Tom checked to make sure Mrs. Rialto couldn't see him. Then he took a length of thread and broke it off. He crept toward the dog and carefully, quietly tied the thread around her tail. Then he snuck over to the sleeping cat and tied the other end around its tail. He did the same to the other cats, tying their tails together with about six feet of thread and then running that same thread around some vases and flowerpots on the windowsill. Then he found a rubber band and a few paper clips, which he hid in his jeans pocket.

"Emma," Mrs. Rialto called out a few minutes later. "I'm ready for you!"

Tom dug the music sheets out of Emma's overstuffed backpack. He took them with him and placed them on the piano.

"What are we going to play today, dear?" Mrs. Rialto asked.

Tom nervously flipped through the sheet music. He couldn't understand any of it. "Uh . . . you know . . . just the usual."

"Let me check your assignment sheet. Yes, I see you have some Mozart for me. And how is that Elton John/Shania Twain duet coming along? You were so excited about that!"

"I was?" said Tom. "I mean . . . yeah, it's going great."

"Then let's get started." Mrs. Rialto ran her hands over the piano keys.

"My mom gave me your check," Tom blurted out.

"Now *that* is truly music to my ears," she said.

Tom pulled the wrinkled check out of his pants pocket.

"It's all mangled," Mrs. Rialto said sourly. "Emma! That's so unlike you. I hope the bank will still take it."

"They probably will if you smooth it out a little."

"I suppose that might help." Mrs. Rialto took the check over to her desk. Once she turned her back to him, Tom pulled out his rubber band. With his thumb and forefinger, he formed a slingshot. He aimed the paper clip and shot it through the kitchen doorway. It smacked Millie right in the butt.

But nothing happened. The dog sat up for a second and looked around, but she didn't run or even bark. In fact, she didn't do anything.

Oh, great! thought Tom. *A lazy dog!*

Mrs. Rialto came back to the piano. "All right, Emma. Let's start with your finger exercises."

Tom frantically untangled his fingers from the rubber band. He reluctantly lifted them onto the keys. Mrs. Rialto opened the music book and began to count. "And a one, and a two, and a . . ."

But suddenly something did happen in the kitchen. A cat yowled and hissed. Then Tom heard the sound of the dog's claws scraping loudly on the linoleum floor.

Mrs. Rialto jumped when she heard a large crash. "What could that be?" She got up to investigate and went into the waiting room. "My little darlings! What have you done!"

As soon as she was out of sight, Tom reloaded his slingshot. He aimed at a different cat that had wandered out of the waiting room. He missed, but the cat darted for the stairs and attracted the attention of Millie, who darted across the floor, pulling some other cat's tail behind her.

This set off a great chain reaction. Vases and flowerpots began falling everywhere.

"Bernice!" cried Mrs. Rialto.

Tom then snuck over to one of the birdcages and let out a canary. At first, the bird wouldn't fly. Tom waved at it. "Move your fat butt!" The canary became frightened and fluttered out of the cage in the direction of the kitchen. When Millie saw the bird, things really got crazy. Tom had never seen a dog run so fast or jump so high. Millie almost caught the canary in midair. She probably would have if she hadn't had a cat tied to her tail.

"*Ahhhhhhhh!*" Mrs. Rialto shrieked when she saw the fiasco. "My cats! My dog! My *birds!*"

The poor canary, having just avoided being chomped by the dog, escaped into the living room. The dog ran after it, bounding across the floor, dragging the cat backward across the carpet. The cat managed to sink its claws into a curtain, and in a moment, an entire set of drapes came tumbling down, covering an aquarium, among other things.

"My *fish!*" Mrs. Rialto screamed.

"Move your fat butt!" a parrot squawked.

As for Tom, he had returned to the piano bench, where he pretended to be upset that this distraction was keeping him from his beloved finger exercises.

"What are you doing?" bellowed Mrs. Rialto. "Help me!"

"But what about my duet?" said Tom.

Mrs. Rialto didn't answer. She was too busy trying to catch the dog.

"Move your fat butt!" repeated the parrot. The other cats were now running around, frightened by the commotion. Millie bounded from couch to coffee table, knocking over lamps, dishes, and picture frames. The cat, still being dragged along behind Millie, yowled with all its might, and in one final attempt to stop itself, sank its claws into the bottom of Mrs. Rialto's skirt. The skirt ripped up and sideways so that Mrs. Rialto's rather enormous granny panties were now on full display.

"Fat butt! Awwwk! Fat butt!" cried the parrot, which was Tom's thought exactly. The other thought was: music lessons weren't so bad. Maybe he'd sign up for some. In the meantime, it was probably best to go. Mrs. Rialto had run upstairs, her hands over her enormous backside. Millie was eating a couch cushion. One of the cats was hanging by its tail from one of the birdcages.

Tom's work here was done.

EMMA GOES FOR A RIDE

Once Tom was gone, Emma was alone at school. It was a strange sensation for her: nobody to pick her up and nobody expecting her anywhere. While a part of her felt uneasy, another part of her felt good. She was finally free. She didn't have to answer to anyone. For once she could do what she wanted.

Emma slung Tom's nearly empty backpack over her shoulder and began walking in the general direction of Tom's house. She wasn't used to being by herself, wandering down the street. She passed the old Whitman house. People always talked about how creepy the Whitmans were and all the junk they had in their backyard. But Emma had never seen it herself—she was always on the bus. Now she could walk right up to the fence and peer in. . . .

Smack! A dirt clod exploded in front of Emma and she

jumped back. Another one whizzed by her head. *Who's attacking me?* she thought as she ducked to the ground.

But it wasn't an attack. It was just Dustin Fletcher, Zach, and some other boys from school. They pulled up beside her on their bikes.

"What's up?" Dustin asked.

Emma cautiously stood. Apparently this was just how boys said hello.

"I'm walking home," she said.

"Wanna check out Food Plus?"

The grocery store? "I can't," Emma said. "I, uh, I have to go home."

"Go home? Why?"

"I have stuff I have to do."

"Like what?" said Zach. *"Homework?"*

The boys all laughed. Emma didn't get why homework was so funny.

"Food Plus just got a delivery of *sweet* new shopping carts. You know, those really big ones," Dustin said.

"Yeah!" said Zach. "They're bigger than Costco. They're like the Hummers of shopping carts."

Dustin smirked. "They got huge wheels with big high-tech shock absorbers."

"That's . . . nice." Emma had no idea what they were talking about.

"So you're coming with us, right?"

"I don't think so," she said. "My family doesn't really shop at Food Plus. . . ."

The boys cracked up again. Zach did an impersonation

of her as a rich snob. "My *fah-mily* doesn't really *shaawp* at Food Plus." Everyone thought this was hilarious, except for Emma.

"We're not talking about your *family*, Tom," said Dustin. "We're talking about *you*."

"Well, I'd like to, really, it sounds great, but I—"

"Dude, you're coming," said Dustin. "No excuses. Let's go!"

"But I—" She tried to interrupt, but no one was listening. One of the boys grabbed her backpack and started riding away. Another boy stopped and motioned to her to get on the back of his bike. She reluctantly got on. *Food Plus, here I come*, she thought.

In the grocery-store parking lot, Zach and Dustin found one of the new shopping carts. It was much bigger than a normal one, but so what? Emma watched while they took turns riding in it and pushing it. When it was Emma's turn to ride, they all seemed to get extra excited. Once she was inside it, Dustin pushed her out of the parking lot and down the sidewalk.

Emma remained utterly baffled by this activity. "And why is this fun again?" she asked Dustin over the loud sound of rattling metal.

"You're riding in a shopping cart," Dustin said. "What could be funner than that?"

"And not an old clunky shopping cart," Zach shouted. "That baby's the Hummer of shopping carts!"

"So I've heard," Emma said. Her mother would be furious if she could see this. She was always very conscientious about returning carts to the cart corral.

Dustin pushed her onto Kenniwick Avenue. Although the shopping cart had "high-tech shock absorbers," it was still a noisy, shaky ride, even on Kenniwick Avenue, which was fairly flat.

"Shouldn't I be wearing a safety helmet or something?" yelled Emma. They seemed to be going faster now, and the other boys were riding beside her on their bikes.

"A safety helmet?" Dustin yelled. "What are you? A girl?"

As a matter of fact . . .

"This thing can't tip over," Zach shouted from his bike. "It has special stabilizers. It's the Hum—"

"I know, I know. It's the Hummer of shopping carts." Emma was getting worried. Her teeth were rattling. "I think that's enough," she yelled to Dustin. "Why don't I push you for a while?"

"But I don't want to ride!" he yelled. "I like to push!"

Emma saw that they were veering slightly to the left. They were leaving Kenniwick Avenue and turning down . . . *Lott Street*. Lott Street was the steepest road in their neighborhood. And they weren't even slowing down!

"Uh, you guys . . . ?" Emma muttered.

But it was too late. With a sinking feeling Emma realized this had been the point all along. The cart was going too fast for her to jump out.

"Um, you guys?" she shrieked one last time into the wind, not caring whether she sounded like Tom or not.

They pushed her to the edge of Lott Street. Emma gripped the front of the cart in terror. There was no way they were going to push her down it. They couldn't. They wouldn't.

They did.

Lott Street went straight down for about thirty yards and then turned up a small hill on the other side. At the bottom, there was a rickety bridge over Dairy Creek. Lott Street itself was quite lovely. It was lined with trees and flowers. A pretty little picket fence ran along one side. Someone had planted a lush vegetable garden on the other.

Yes, Lott Street was quite nice, thought Emma. *Unless you were about to die!*

The shopping cart picked up speed instantly. Emma had no choice but to crouch into the crash position and try to ride it out. Halfway down Lott Street, the front wheel hit a rock and the cart veered toward a parked car on the right. Then it hit another rock and veered back to the left. It hit a pothole and nearly threw Emma out. She tried to steer by throwing her weight to either side. She just avoided a gravel patch and then nicked the side of a pickup truck.

But by the time she reached the bottom of the hill, the cart was completely out of control. Emma gripped the metal basket until her hands turned white. The cart began to veer again, this time to the right. Emma said a silent prayer and said good-bye to her family, her friends, and her body, wherever it was. . . .

The cart flew off the road and into a yard, flattened a wire garden fence, took out someone's hanging laundry, and plowed into a sprinkler. It bounced once, bounced again, and flipped over—throwing Emma out in the process. She hit the ground with a hard thud and watched while the cart tumbled end over end and finally crashed into the creek.

Emma blinked a few times. Was she still alive? She lifted her head from the grass. Around her there was the sudden sound of dirt bikes skidding to a stop. Hands grabbed her, lifted her up, and brushed her off.

"Tom, dude! That was awesome!"

"How did you do that escape move?"

"Bro, you rule!"

Emma blinked. She *was* still alive. Someone ran to the creek's edge. "That cart is toast. It's like totally underwater!"

"You totally rode that!"

"You shredded!"

"I'm next!" yelled Zach.

"No way," Dustin protested. "I'm going next!"

"Let's do two at a time!" said someone else.

"Let's do a train!"

In their excitement they completely forgot about Emma and hopped back on their bikes.

Emma got to her feet, her legs still shaking, and watched the other boys race up the hill toward Food Plus.

For a moment, she was grateful. She was still alive. Then a darker thought filled her brain. It was a very simple thought: *I hate boys. I hate boys. I hate* all boys!

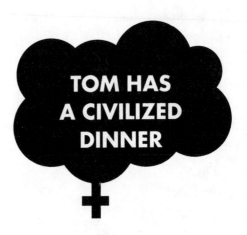

TOM HAS A CIVILIZED DINNER

When Tom arrived at Emma's house after the piano lesson, he snuck upstairs to her bedroom. He'd been there before, back in fourth grade. Unfortunately, it looked pretty much the same. You were supposed to become cooler as you got older. Not dorkier. Poor Emma.

But he had bigger problems to think about. He picked up Emma's phone, sat down on the bed, and punched in his cell number.

"What do you want?" Emma snapped, answering on the first ring.

"What do you think I want?" Tom whispered. "I want to switch back. Where are you?"

"At your house. I'm about to call the police."

"The police? What for?"

"Attempted murder. Your *friends*, Dustin and Zach, put

me in a shopping cart and pushed me down Lott Street! By some miracle, I'm still alive."

"Oh," Tom said, lying back and trying not to feel too jealous. "Well, actually, I pushed Dustin down that same street last week. He kind of owed me."

"What? You've done that to someone? Then you're a psycho too!"

"You're totally safe in those Food Plus carts," Tom insisted. "They have high-tech stabilizers. They're the Hummers of—"

"I know, I know! What's wrong with you? Are all boys insane?"

"Hey, your piano teacher isn't exactly a picture of mental health, you know."

"Oh my God. What did you do to Mrs. Rialto? If you get me in trouble, so help me—"

Tom tried to change the subject. "And what's with your room? It looks like the room of a nine-year-old."

"Nothing's wrong with it. And you leave everything alone. And if you start snooping around—"

"Keep your skirt on. I'm not going to do anything," he said. But the idea of snooping was tempting. He pulled open the top drawer of her bedside table. "How are you doing otherwise? Are you handling my family okay?"

"There's no one here. What about my mom? Has she noticed anything?" she asked.

"I don't think so. I'm hiding out in your room at the moment." He poked through her stuff. There wasn't anything good, only a bottle of something called Zit-B-Gone.

"Maybe we should just tell them," Emma said. "You're not supposed to keep secrets from your parents."

Tom had thought about this too. "Yeah, but what would that do besides freak everyone out? I think we should wait, at least a couple more hours. Maybe we'll switch back tonight, you know, if we get a good night's sleep."

"But by then I might get killed! It's dangerous being a boy!"

"Well, how do you think I feel?" Tom said. "I almost had to play an Elton John duet!"

Tom heard a knock on the door. "Dinner's ready," called Claire.

"Coming," he yelled. He still couldn't get used to his squeaky Minnie Mouse voice.

A few minutes later, Tom sat down at the Bakers' dining room table. Dinner was not usually a big deal at the Witherspoons'—Tom pretty much just grabbed for the good stuff before Ricky got it. Here, Mr. Baker, Claire, and Tom all sat around a carefully set table. There were crystal glasses, shiny silverware, and cloth napkins, which everyone put in their laps. A pot roast and several other dishes were brought out on fine china. Tom began to worry when he saw a big bowl of unidentified green vegetables. Obviously there would be no hickory BBQ potato chips, which was his favorite side dish.

Mrs. Baker placed a gravy boat on the table and took her seat. "Now, this is a new mushroom-Brie cream sauce I'm trying. So everyone tell me what you think."

Tom already knew what he thought: the sauce looked like snot. But he kept it to himself.

"Napkin, Emma," Mrs. Baker said, lifting a sculpted eyebrow. Tom seized his napkin and jammed it in his lap.

"How was school today?" Mr. Baker asked Tom.

"Fine," he replied, and passed a basket of bread from Mrs. Baker to Claire. Claire was wearing black fingernail polish. What a weird family.

"What about health class?" Mrs. Baker asked. She shoveled a huge glob of the greenish vegetable goo onto Tom's plate. "Didn't you say you were doing gender differences this week?"

Tom swallowed hard. Emma actually told her parents what she did in *health class*? "Oh, yeah, we are. It's the funniest thing. It turns out the reason girls are so ridicu—" Mrs. Baker and Claire both stared at him intently. ". . . ridiculously smarter than boys is because that's part of their gender."

Mr. Baker frowned slightly.

Tom looked at the steaming green crud on his plate. At home he was never forced to eat such things without at least being allowed to sprinkle Cocoa Puffs on them first.

"Are you going to pass anything," Claire asked, "or are you just going to sit there with that stupid look on your face?"

"Claire!" Mrs. Baker said.

"But Mom, she's just sitting there. It's like she completely forgot her manners."

"Well, don't forget yours," Mrs. Baker scolded.

The focus returned to Tom. "How about that math assignment?" asked Mr. Baker. "What did your teacher think of your fractions worksheet?"

"My fractions worksheet?" Tom repeated. "Oh. Uh . . . she liked it. She liked it a lot. She likes fractions anyway. I mean, even if you get one wrong. Fractions are her favorite. Two thirds, one seventh. She loves that stuff."

"You got one wrong?" Mrs. Baker said.

"Oh no," said Tom, shaking his head. "No. I got 'em all right. One hundred percent. Just like always. She even used mine to grade the other worksheets. Fractions, decimals, percents. Got 'em all. A-plus, you know me."

"How about your report on Venezuela?" Mr. Baker asked. "Did Mrs. Shaw have any comments?"

Venezuela? Tom stuffed a piece of bread in his mouth to buy time. But it didn't help. Everyone waited for him to finish. This was exhausting. How did Emma deal with all this pressure? "She dinks iz really good," he said with his mouth full.

"Did she like the extra research you included from that article on the wild chimp problem in *National Geographic?*"

"Totally." Tom swallowed hard. "She thought that was the best part. She said the wild monkeys are really getting bad. You know, eating all the bananas and stealing tricycles and diapers and stuff."

"Could we please talk about something other than wild monkeys and diapers?" Claire said.

"Wild monkeys are no laughing matter," Mr. Baker told her. "They're a real problem in South America."

"*Yeah,* Claire!" said Tom. "They're a serious problem! Just look in *National Geographic.*"

Mrs. Baker suddenly swooped down with a spoonful of

72

the dreadful mushroom-Brie sauce. "Here, Emma. Taste this for me." Then she thrust the spoon toward Tom's mouth.

Tom was caught off guard and had no choice but to accept it. It was in his mouth before he could stop her.

What followed was a little messy. Tom did not exactly puke the mushroom-Brie sauce up. It was more like an involuntary gag response. It was a good thing he had his napkin in his lap, because that was where most of it went.

But it all worked out for the best. Once he'd gagged all over himself, Tom was excused from dinner and free of any more school questions. He was given a can of seltzer water and four Pepto-Bismol tablets and sent to the den, which was what the Bakers called their TV room. The Bakers' dog, Gunner, liked the Pepto tablets and ate them all in one bite.

It was the second time that day that a strange dog had helped Tom out. He just hoped Emma had found someone to help her too.

EMMA DINES WITHERSPOON STYLE

Emma was enjoying an equally unusual dinner at Tom's house. The first course had been Kraft macaroni and cheese with tuna fish (which actually was quite tasty). The second course was some green beans, which had been nuked in the microwave (also not bad, and she and Ricky were allowed to dip them in extraspicy barbecue sauce). Now, for dessert, she was polishing off a large bowl of half Cap'n Crunch, half Froot Loops, while she and Ricky watched *America's Funniest Home Videos*. Ricky was being obnoxious, making farting noises and crushing Froot Loops on the coffee table with a paperweight. And then Mrs. Witherspoon joined them. She flopped on the couch and laughed with Emma and Ricky when a baby on TV got stuck in a doggy door.

Emma had to admit, the Witherspoon way of doing

things had its own unique charms. Still, she worried about Mrs. Witherspoon. She'd always been kind of quirky, but ever since the divorce she had seemed just plain sad.

But Emma could not afford to worry about other people. She had urgent work to do. As soon as *America's Funniest* was over, she excused herself and went upstairs to Tom's computer.

First, she Googled "body switches." Since Tom's computer didn't have any blocks on it, several sites of naked women popped up. Did boys do anything except look at naked girls and try to kill each other? Apparently not.

Next, she searched for "magic," "supernatural phenomenon," and "body switching." A promising Web site popped up: mythsandcursesofthepacificnorthwest.com.

The Tohaka Love Curse

The Tohakas, an Eskimo tribe, made their home in the barren ice fields of northwestern Canada. According to legend, a newly married couple built a house on a remote ice field. But the man was from a family of brothers and did not understand women. The woman was from a family of sisters and did not understand men. And so they argued constantly.

The Tohaka god Winnihecket was the god of the ice fields and the great waters. He liked to sleep, and so preferred quiet. Once this couple arrived, their constant bickering ruined the silence for miles in every direction. Even the birds and the fish were driven away.

75

So Winnihecket placed a curse on a common arrowhead, which he slipped into the man's clothing. That night, in the midst of their nightly arguments, they both reached for the same piece of fish and knocked heads, momentarily knocking each other out. When they awoke, they had switched bodies. This was how Winnihecket hoped to teach them to understand and respect the opposite sex. If they could not learn to co-operate in an honest and open way, he would leave them in each other's bodies forever. He gave them four days, since four was the Tohakas' sacred number.

When the couple learned of the curse, they tried not to argue. But every time they spoke, a new fight started. Finally they decided to speak nicely out loud and argue only in sign language. The silence was thus preserved, and soon the fish and birds came back. Winnihecket was greatly relieved. He reversed the curse and went back to sleep.

The couple never exchanged a cross word after that, though they became excellent at arguing in sign language. Once, during a heated argument, the woman used her middle finger to tell her husband he was as useless as a single snow pigeon, which is why even in modern times, the angry extension of the middle finger is known as "flipping the bird."

Emma's heart began to race. A curse? An arrowhead? Tom had had an arrowhead on the bus!

She printed out the Tohaka legend and read it again.

This Eskimo couple were very similar to her and Tom, not counting the fact that they were married Eskimos. But how exactly did they switch back? By learning to argue in silence? Or was learning to get along and actually understanding each other the key to reversing the curse?

She sent Tom an instant message.

Flowerpower: are you there? i found something major.

Tomthemoose: flowerpower??????????????

Flowerpower: shut up and listen. meet me at the tree house tomorrow b4 school. big news.

Tomthemoose: OK. See U there.

Emma clicked off and read the curse again. They only had four days, one of which was almost over.

TOM'S FIRST NAKED GIRL

On Thursday morning, Tom woke up in Emma's pastel sheets. Her room looked different in the daylight, more pink. He checked the clock. He had to meet Emma at the tree fort soon.

Someone pounded on the door. "You have three minutes for your shower!" yelled Claire. "The clock starts now!"

Tom dragged himself out of bed. Last night, he'd put on some pajamas he found in a drawer. Now he dug through Emma's closet for a robe and a towel.

He went into the bathroom, locked the door, and turned on the shower. As he pulled off his pajama top he glanced into the mirror and saw *a girl taking off her pajamas*. Yowza! He'd been too tired to check this out the night before, but what an opportunity. He made sure the door was locked and went back to the sink. He stood in front of the mirror, but he could only see Emma's body from the waist up. He stood on top of the toilet so he could get the whole picture. He turned in the mirror and checked out his profile. He stuck out his chest, puckered his lips, and pouted like supermodels did. Then he tried moving his hips from side to side. *Yee-haw!* He pulled his pajama top down his shoulder. *Hot bod!* Then he did a little striptease, unbuttoning his pajama top, one button at a time. . . .

"One minute!" screamed Claire through the door. "And you better not be wasting time *admiring* yourself in the mirror!"

Tom nearly fell off the toilet. How did she know? Had she seen him somehow? He yanked off his pajamas and hurried into the shower. He'd gawk at Emma's body later.

But once he was in the water, he had a new problem. *What did girls do in here?* He felt his long thick hair. There was so much of it. Should he wash it? Would it ever dry? And where were the soap and washcloths? All he could find was a scratchy sponge thing and bottles of stuff with names like Nutrique Body Wash, Apple Blossom Noncarb Preconditioner, and Ultimus Body Exfoliating Sensitizer.

"Thirty seconds!"

Tom picked up one of the bottles. What was Exfoliating Sensitizer? And where was the soap?

After a quick and confusing shower experience, Tom got dressed and then hurried off into the woods. He crawled up the tree fort ladder, marveling at how light and agile Emma's body was. Once he was up there, he looked at his watch. He was actually on time. But where was Emma?

While he waited, he sat down on the square of old carpet that was still on the floor. It had gotten kind of moldy in the last year. When the fort was built, he and Brad wouldn't let Emma help at first, but she kept hanging around and eventually they relented. In the end, it was Emma, not Brad, who became Tom's true partner. The first time they slept there, Brad got scared of the dark and the sounds in the woods, so he went home. Emma and Tom had been scared too, but they'd stayed together and stuck it out until the sun came up. Tom remembered the way Emma breathed when she finally fell asleep. He remembered thinking he would always protect her if he could. Not in some sappy way, but because she was a girl, and kind of small, and had been loyal to him by helping out. . . .

"Hey!" a voice shouted. "Who's up there?"

Tom woke up from his daydream and peered down below. It was Zach Leland.

Tom caught himself before he said his own name. "Emma. Emma Baker."

"Whaddaya doing in that tree house?" Zach asked.

"Nothing."

"You can't be up there, you're a girl."

"So what," Tom said. "It's my tree house."

"That isn't yours. That's Tom Witherspoon's."

"I helped him build it," Tom squeaked.

Zach put down his backpack and picked up a dirt clod. He threw it at Tom. "Get outta there, Toadstool."

Tom ducked as the dirt clod flew past. "Yeah?" he said to Zach. "Well, why don't you come up here and make me?"

"What?"

"Are you deaf? I said, *make me.*"

"I can't fight you," Zach said. "You're a girl."

"So then shut up."

Zach seemed confused by this logic. He stood staring up at the tree house. Then another small dirt clod whizzed through the air, this one aimed at Zach. It missed his head by six inches.

Zach stumbled backward. "Whoaa!"

Emma appeared. She had a big chunk of dirt in her hand and it was cocked back threateningly. Tom was impressed. In his body, Emma could really throw. For a moment, he thought about baseball tryouts, which were that night. He had assumed he would have to forfeit his chance to make A team, or any team, for that matter. But if Emma was that accurate, maybe she could do his tryouts for him.

"What are you mad at me for?" cried Zach. "I'm trying to get that girl out of your tree house!"

"Leave her alone." Emma did her best Tom-the-tough-guy voice. "I told her to meet me here."

"You did? Why'd you do that?"

"Why don't you go beat up some fourth graders or something," Tom said from the tree house.

A baffled Zach watched the two of them and backed away. "Jeez," he grumbled. "I was just trying to help a guy out."

When Zach was gone, Tom huddled with Emma in the tree house. Emma flattened the Tohaka love curse printouts on the floor. Then Tom noticed Emma staring at him.

"Oh my God, what did you do to my hair?" Emma asked as she reached out and touched Tom's head.

"Nothing," Tom said defensively. "I washed it."

"But it's all gooey . . . and stuck together. I look like Bozo the Clown!"

"Well, don't blame me. I just did what it said on the bottle."

"Which bottle?"

"The Fresh and Smooth hair stuff."

"What? That's not for *cleaning* hair. That's for getting *rid* of it! Tom! You idiot! I'm going to go bald!"

"It's not my fault you have three hundred bottles of crap in your shower!"

"Well, you can read a label, can't you?"

"How can I when your stupid sister is screaming at me every fifteen seconds?"

Emma sighed. "All right, all right, we'll deal with the hair later. Now take a look at this."

Tom bent over the papers and read about the Tohaka love curse. Emma sat beside him and read along. "Wow," Tom said. "This does sound like us. Do you think this is what happened?"

"It's possible. And didn't you have an arrowhead on the bus on Tuesday?"

"I did. And I found it by the old Klickitat settlement. Do you think the Klickitat could be related to the Tohaka?"

She showed him a different printout with a map of North American trade routes. "Remember what we learned in social studies?"

"No." Tom had never learned anything in social studies.

"Mrs. Shaw said that all the tribes from this area were related," Emma explained. "They traveled up and down the coast. To trade stuff."

"Wow," said Tom. "Something from school that's actually useful!"

"Lots of things from school are useful, if you give them a chance," Emma said while folding up the papers. "But first things first. Where's that arrowhead?"

"Good question." Tom strained to think. "I found it in the woods . . . I put it in my pocket . . . then I showed it to Brad . . . who showed me his drawing of the new music teacher. . . . It was one of his better drawings. . . . It showed her from a side view—"

"The arrowhead?" Emma asked impatiently.

"Right, right . . . it was in my pocket, in my cargo pants . . . and then the trampoline . . . That's right! When I got on the trampoline I stuck it in the ankle pocket of my cargo pants!" Tom said. "And then we switched, so you would have it. It must still be in those pants."

"Oh," said Emma. "I put those in the wash."

Tom glared at her. "What? You *washed* my cargo pants? I never wash those! That's where I keep everything."

"Don't worry, your Gummi worms are safe," Emma said. "But what about this curse? Do you think we fit the rest of it?"

"Well, we're not married," he said.

"No."

"We aren't Eskimos."

"No."

"But we do kinda hate each other."

"Yeah."

"And we definitely argue a lot."

"We argue all the time," Emma agreed. "But it's not like we're disturbing the silence of the ice fields."

Tom scratched his head. "The important thing is we're a boy and a girl and we fight all the time. We also had the arrowhead with us. That *must* be what happened."

Emma nodded. "I think you're right. But how exactly do we use the arrowhead to change back?"

"We just do what it says. We argue in sign language or whatever." Tom pretended to do some sign language. He gave Emma a thumbs-up and then a thumbs-down. Then he made the gesture of the snow pigeon.

"Stop it. It must be more complicated than that. It sounds like we're supposed to learn to understand each other," said Emma. "And actually get along. Don't you think?"

Tom frowned. This was starting to sound like a homework problem. Emma was better at stuff like that. "Well, the first thing is to get those cargo pants out of the wash," he said. "If Ricky finds the arrowhead, we're toast."

Emma put the papers in her pocket. Then a troubled look came over her face. Tom knew it was something serious because it was the same face he had made when his parents had told him they were getting divorced. "Tom?" she said.

"Yeah?"

"What you said before . . . we don't really hate each other, do we?"

Tom shrugged. "I don't know. I don't hate you."

"I don't hate you either."

"Of course you do," Tom said. "The Grrlzillas and all that?"

"Courtney's the real Grrlzilla. And even she likes boys a little."

Tom crawled over to the ladder. "All I know is we need to get that arrowhead before Ricky finds it."

"Tom?" Emma said. "Can I ask you one more thing?"

"What?"

"How come we stopped being friends?"

"How would I know?"

"Did I do something?"

"No," Tom said. "We just got older. You can't be friends with girls in sixth grade."

"Why not?"

"Because. Girls get weird in sixth grade. They start to want things."

"But I don't want anything," said Emma. "And I miss being friends."

Tom stopped midrung. "We have to get ourselves out of this mess. Then we can, uh, figure that other stuff out." Because if he had to admit it, he missed being friends too.

THE FINER POINTS OF SLACKING

With barely fifteen minutes left until school started, Emma ran back to her house to get the arrowhead out of the wash. She would never risk being late as herself, but she was Tom Witherspoon now. It wasn't like anyone was going to notice.

At Tom's house, she dashed downstairs and quickly dug through the laundry basket. Although Tom's mother wasn't much of a cook, she seemed to be good at cleaning. Emma found the cargo pants folded neatly on a table with Tom's other clean clothes. She searched the ankle pocket. No arrowhead.

She found a shoe box where Mrs. Witherspoon apparently emptied the contents of Tom's pockets. Everything else was there—the plastic eyeball, the skateboard wheel, the Gummi worms—everything but the arrowhead. Emma yanked open the door of the dryer and rummaged around inside it. She opened the washer and peered inside. She scoured the lint tray and the garbage can. She checked under the table, under some chairs, under the washer, under everything she could think of.

"Looking for this?" Emma spun around. Ricky had snuck down the stairs behind her and now held up the arrowhead in his grimy hand. Its smooth gray surface glinted in the sunlight.

Emma studied the little boy carefully. "Nope," she said. "I wasn't."

Ricky looked confused. "You sure? It's pretty cool."

"That thing? I bought that for a quarter. You can have it," Emma said. "What I really need are those Gummi worms."

"What do you want those for?"

"Nothing. Just a little . . . experiment."

"What experiment?"

"It's for big kids. Nothing you'd be interested in." Emma nonchalantly stuck the shoe box on an out-of-reach shelf and pretended to search the laundry room.

"What is it?" Ricky said, forgetting the arrowhead. "Tell me! Tell me!"

"Well," Emma said with a sigh, "these guys at school told me if you put Gummi worms in water, then add some salt and a little lemon juice, they start to swell up. And if you put them under a hot light, they get so big they fill up a whole glass. It looks like brains, mushed into a jar."

Ricky's eyes opened wide. Lucky for Emma, Tom had

told her that the only thing Ricky loved more than ninjas and sword fights was stuff that looked like brains. Especially *mushed* brains.

"Can I see?" Ricky asked. "If I help you find them?"

"I dunno." Emma acted as if she were looking under the washer. "It's really for older kids. I wouldn't want to scare you, or give you nightmares."

"I won't get nightmares!" Ricky insisted. He put the arrowhead on the counter and began scrambling around the laundry room, looking for the candy. "I swear I won't. I saw a dead possum once and there were ants and little wormy things all over it."

"That's not really the same."

"Its guts were falling out and it smelled terrible and we took it to William's house and put it in a box!"

Emma tried not to barf. "All right, you can help. But first we gotta find the Gummis. They're not in here, so where could they be?"

Ricky ran into the storage room and began digging wildly through the junk there. Emma smoothly scooped up the arrowhead, crept back toward the stairs, and ran to school.

Unfortunately, with all the other things on her mind, Emma had not really thought about the complications school might create. Her first problem was Tom's locker combination. She also didn't know his schedule, where he sat, or what his assignments were.

Nor was she prepared to be thoroughly ignored by his teachers. In third-period science, Mr. Gibbons wouldn't call on her. She raised her hand for each question, and each time, he called on someone else. When she finally blurted out one of the answers, Mr. Gibbons just laughed as if it were a joke. And it was the right answer! But because she was Tom now, no one listened to anything she said. It was really frustrating.

Emma learned other things too. For instance, all the boys in the back row slept through social studies. It was expected. The teacher actually looked at her funny when he saw that she was wide awake.

There was also an ongoing spitball fight during math class. She figured this out because she kept getting pelted in the back of the head so thoroughly that she spent the rest of the day picking spitballs out of her hair.

At each class change, she had to run down the hall to find Tom. They desperately exchanged information about each other's classes on a need-to-know basis and ran back to their lockers. It was all very complicated and difficult.

Finally, after lunch, Emma caught a break. Tom had art, which was his easiest class of the day. She went to the long table by the window and sat with Zach, a guy named Owen, Brad, and Jeff Matthews. Emma tried to distract herself with the day's art assignment, which was to make a clay sculpture. She wanted a better look at the arrowhead anyway, so she took it out and began to construct a model of it with her clay.

The other boys worked with their clay and listened

while Jeff talked. "So I'm at the mall," Jeff began. "And this girl comes up to me. She obviously liked me. But I'm like, you're kinda short. I'm more into tall chicks. And she's like, I could stand on a stool if you want. I was like, nah, but you got any tall friends?"

The boys loved this. They leaned closer to hear what happened next. Emma did too.

Jeff went on. "And so then her friend comes over and she's a little taller but with brown hair. And she's like, want to come over and play video games? My parents don't get home till later. And I'm like, nah, I kinda prefer blondes. You got any blond friends?"

"Genius," Owen said, nudging Brad.

"You told a brown-haired girl you only liked blondes? That's awesome," said Brad.

"And so then this other chick comes over," Jeff continued. "And this one's seriously hot. Which was my plan all along . . . to wait for the really hot one. So she's like, do you think you're too good for my friends? And I'm like, those other girls weren't up to my standards. And she's like, I'm not sure you're up to *my* standards, and I'm like, girl, I *am* your standard!"

The boys all laughed loudly.

"You totally know how to handle girls," said Zach.

"See, the thing with girls is," Jeff whispered to the table, "you can sweet-talk 'em a little. Give 'em a little of that romantic girly crap. But you never give in. Always make sure they know who's boss."

"You're so right!" Brad said.

"That's the way to do it," Zach said.

Emma kept her head down. Was Jeff really this slimy?

"What about your other girlfriend?" Zach asked.

"Yeah," Brad said. "That girl you met two weeks ago?"

But Jeff didn't feel like answering. He was making a race car with his clay and driving it around on the table. Brad was making a naked girl. Zach had flattened his clay into a pancake and was stabbing it with a pencil. Owen was attempting a baseball bat. *Chimpanzees are more artistic*, thought Emma.

Then Mrs. Rosenberg, the art teacher, appeared. "Look at Tom's piece," she said. "Is that an arrowhead? What lovely flower carvings." She leaned over and studied the arrowhead model Emma had made. Actually, it wasn't a model at all, it was the arrowhead itself, covered with clay. Emma had carved some vines and flowers onto the top of it.

Once Mrs. Rosenberg was gone, Owen began to snicker. "*Flower carvings?*"

"You're doing flower carvings?" Brad asked.

"And you call me a wuss!" said Zach.

"Those aren't flowers," Emma said, trying to defend herself. "They're dragons!"

"They're toast now!" said Jeff. He reached over and pounded Emma's sculpture with his fist, destroying it. When Brad saw this, he reached over and smashed Jeff's race car. Zach squished Brad's naked girl, and then all the boys began pounding each other's sculptures until every bit of clay was squashed flat.

"Hey, check this out." Jeff grabbed all the clay and threw

the lump on the floor. "What's the last thing some loser dude sees who tries to mess with me?"

He stomped on the clay with his foot. When Jeff lifted his shoe there was a large imprint of a Nike Swoosh in the clay. The boys carried on as if this were the most hilarious thing they'd ever seen.

Emma was horrified. The arrowhead was in there! Fortunately, the minute the bell rang, all the boys ran for the door. Emma immediately dropped to the floor and began stabbing at the clay mound with her plastic knife. Could you break the arrowhead? Would it still work if you did? Her knife hit something hard. She clawed through the clay with her fingernails, finally uncovering the arrowhead. She pried it out of the clay as the next class came in. When she finally stood up, seventh- and eighth-grade boys had already surrounded her.

"Dawg," said one. "It's Tom the Mack Daddy!"

"He doesn't look like much, but this bro gets girls!"

"Hey, Tom. Where's Emma Baker? Gettin' any closet action today?"

They all laughed loudly. Emma stood there and turned red from embarrassment.

One of the boys saw the arrowhead. "Whatcha got there, Tom? Is that for Emma? You gonna ask her to go steady?"

"Hey, why bother?" said a blond kid with braces. "She'll make out with you anyway!"

Emma could barely contain the impulse to kick them all in the shins. Instead, she forced a smile and walked calmly to the door.

She stepped on the foot of the blond kid, just by accident, of course. With all that extra Tom weight, and with a little bit of a *stomp* added to it, it seemed to hurt the boy quite a bit. He was still yowling in pain as Emma hurried to her next class.

TOM GETS AN EYEFUL

Meanwhile, Tom was having school problems of his own. Just like Emma, he was going to the wrong classes, sitting in the wrong seats, and going into the wrong bathroom. None of which would have been too unusual if he had been good old Tom Witherspoon. But people expected more of Emma Baker.

"What can you tell us about Mount Rushmore, Emma?" Mr. Beatty asked.

Tom quickly glanced around the room. Everyone was staring. "Uh, wasn't Bill Murray in that?"

Mr. Beatty looked puzzled and called on someone else.

The whole day was like that. Tom was the first person teachers called on. They asked him about decimal points. Africa. The forms of democratic government. They asked him about chemical compounds and how to say "I drink my coffee in the restaurant" in Spanish. Tom's joke—"Why don't they just go to Starbucks?"—didn't go over at all. Apparently Emma wasn't very funny.

Tom struggled through his first three periods and was greatly relieved when fourth-period PE class arrived. Nobody would call on him in PE.

He followed Courtney and the other girls into the locker room. That was when he realized what was about to happen. Tom was about to see twenty-five girls completely naked. And then he saw Kelly Angstrom coming in behind him. Could it be? Was it possible? It was: Kelly Angstrom was in his PE class!

But Tom had to be careful. He couldn't draw attention to himself. He calmly walked to Emma's locker while the other girls stripped to their underwear and put on their shorts and gym shirts. Tom tried *not* to stare at what was happening around him. Especially as Kelly was, quite literally, spilling out of her lacy black bra.

On the soccer field, the girls were much better than Tom expected, and without his normal size and strength he could barely keep up. Kelly was especially fierce. She pushed girls down and elbowed them out of the way. At one point, she knocked Tom flat on his back and then laughed at him while she kicked a goal. Tom lay on the ground looking up at her. She was so beautiful, even from the grassy turf.

Then a new thought came to Tom. This was gym. When the game was over, they'd all go inside.

And take *showers.*

When Mrs. Weissman blew her whistle, Tom followed

the other girls back to the locker room. The conversation turned to Jeff Matthews.

"My cousin from Idaho was visiting," said Hannah Lewis. "And I showed her a picture of Jeff and she said at her school they think guys like that are cheesy."

"That's because she doesn't know him," said another girl.

"She doesn't see him every day."

"And if she's from *Idaho* . . ."

"We know how cute he is, don't we, Emma?" Courtney said.

"I don't think he's that cute," Tom said. "I think he's sort of a fake."

All the girls stopped talking.

"*What* did you say?" Courtney asked.

"The only reason everyone likes him is because everyone *else* likes him," Tom said. "Everyone's just copying everybody else."

All the girls were shocked. This seemed to be the most outrageous statement any of them had ever heard. Jeff Matthews's hotness apparently had never been questioned.

"You know what?" Kelly said. "I agree. Liking Jeff Matthews is *sooo* sixth grade. Next year when we're in seventh, there'll be new boys. Boys who aren't so full of themselves."

"But Jeff is gorgeous!" Ashley protested. "Everyone likes Jeff!"

"I *adore* Jeff," said Rachel with authority. Evidently nobody had mentioned to her that Jeff constantly made fun of her braces and called her Armpit Breath.

"And who else is there?" another girl asked. "Brad Hailey? Who draws pictures of us naked?"

"Or Zach Leland?" Ashley said.

"Or Tom Witherspoon?" Courtney added.

"What's so bad about Tom Witherspoon?" Tom asked.

The other girls looked at him like he had lost his marbles.

"Actually," Kelly replied, "I think Tom is sorta cute. You know, in a bumbling, clueless kind of way."

Tom almost swallowed his tongue. Had he heard that right?

"At least he thinks about something besides his clothes and his hair," Kelly said.

Tom noticed that most of the other girls didn't seem convinced. They still thought Jeff was the cutest. But so what? *Kelly Angstrom* had said he was okay. That was what mattered. That and the fact that he was about to get naked with twenty-five sixth-grade girls.

When Tom entered the locker room, the showers were already running. Steam wafted through the air. Tom sat in front of Emma's locker and slowly untied his shoes.

Margaret was first into the shower. Tom looked away quickly—the last thing he wanted was to see Margaret naked. He'd had a quick glance at her candy-stripe underwear and it wasn't a pretty sight.

Then pimply Rachel wrapped a towel around herself and ran past him. Tom didn't want to see that either. When Queen Kong began to strip, he looked in the opposite direction, but then Ashley's big butt ran by, so he closed his eyes. When was this going to get good?

"Hurry up, Emma!" Mrs. Weissman barked. Tom swallowed hard and reached around to unfasten his bra. He tried reaching up his back, but he couldn't get his hand up to unhook the back bra strap. So he tried reaching down from the top. That didn't work either. Right in front of him, Hannah reached up and unfastened her bra with ease. What was his problem? He'd managed to fasten it that morning. He stretched his arm as far as it would go. . . .

"Having trouble, Emma?" said Kelly.

A couple of the other girls giggled.

"Oh no," Tom replied. "It's just . . . my arm, you know, sometimes . . ." He reached as far up his back as he could and touched the strap, but he couldn't get it undone. Brad had once tried to teach Tom the classic "one-hand release" technique. However, Tom had been too busy playing his Game Boy and hadn't paid attention. He regretted that now.

"Want some help with that?" Kelly walked toward him. She was stripped down to her bra and panties.

"Here, hold still," she breathed sexily. Tom felt his knees tremble as she approached. He tried desperately not to stare. When he felt Kelly's hand on his bare back, he nearly fainted.

But she didn't unfasten the bra. She tightened it.

"What did you do?" stammered Tom. He could barely breathe, the bra was so tight.

"Well, you're getting so *developed*," Kelly said in a mocking tone. "You're getting so *big* now. I thought you probably needed a little tightening. You don't want those *huge breasts* of yours falling out."

The locker room filled with laughter. Tom felt himself turning bright red.

And then, while Tom fumbled to release himself, the most shocking thing of all happened. Kelly Angstrom, who was no more than two feet in front of him, slid her hand up her own back, undid her bra, and let it fall gently into her hands.

There she was. Kelly Angstrom. Fully on display.

Tom's eyes nearly popped out of his head. His mouth fell open. Everything he'd ever imagined, everything he'd ever dreamed of. Two round, perfect, bodacious . . .

But it was too much for this sixth-grade boy to digest. Tom's head began to spin.

"What's the matter, Emma?" Kelly asked. "You look a little pale."

Tom tried to walk away, but his legs had turned to rubber. His vision went fuzzy. He felt the room begin to spin. . . .

Fortunately, Mrs. Weissman was there to catch him.

When he woke up later, Tom was on a cot in the gym office, wrapped in a blanket.

"How are you feeling?" Mrs. Weissman asked with concern.

"Okay," said Tom. "Where am I? What happened?"

"You fainted."

"I did?"

"Don't worry. I called your mother. She'll take you home. You're excused for the rest of the day."

Tom sat up on the cot. What was she talking about? He couldn't go home. He had to go back to the locker room. He had to be around Kelly. Kelly liked him. She'd said he was cute!

Then he looked down at his tiny legs and remembered that it didn't matter. Not as long as he was in Emma's body. Tom threw off the blanket and stood up. He had to switch back—*now*—before Kelly started liking someone else.

"Emma!" said Mrs. Weissman. "What are you doing? Lie back down. You're not well."

"But I'm fine, Mrs. Weissman. I need to get back to class," he said.

"No, Emma. You fainted. You need to rest. Your mother is on her way. We need you in top shape for the gymnastics meet on Saturday."

Tom sat back down. That was the thing about being Emma. Every day there was some new activity, some new responsibility. Everyone counted on Emma.

Then another memory came back to him. *Baseball.* Tryouts were tonight! He had to remind Emma to go. He snuck his cell phone out and text-messaged Emma. Of course, she wouldn't be good enough for A team, but at least she could go and get him registered for B team, or C, if need be. Any baseball was better than no baseball. . . .

EMMA NEVER FORGETS

But Emma didn't need any reminding. She had already prepared for baseball tryouts. The night before, Tom's dad had FedExed a box of baseballs to the Witherspoon house. Emma had unpacked them and spent several hours pitching into the large white strike zone painted on the fence. She'd learned pretty quickly how to work Tom's powerful arm.

Emma caught up with Tom on the way to fifth period and told him not to worry. "I'll go to the tryouts and see what I can do. But what about figuring out the arrowhead? Isn't that more important?"

"We can worry about that later," he said. "Just get me on the C team at least. Or the B team if you can manage it."

Emma was annoyed by Tom's attitude. "Tom, I'm good

at sports, remember? Or do you still think gymnastics doesn't count?"

"Just don't suck, okay?" Tom said. "And please, *please* don't do anything weird. Like start crying."

"Tom, I don't suck at things. Okay? I'll be fine. Don't worry."

After school, Emma walked onto the field with Tom's baseball glove in her hand. She didn't like how Tom had spoken to her, but when she saw all the fathers and sons milling around, she wound up feeling sorry for him. When Tom's parents had gotten divorced and his dad had moved out, all the kids had been shaken by it. Tom had been different after that. He became a total jock, playing baseball and throwing himself into competition. Sitting there by herself with Tom's glove in her lap, Emma realized how hard things must have been for him. And who could he really talk to? Boys weren't supportive the way girls were. She had seen it herself. Being a boy was lonely.

Tom's name was called, and Emma walked to the pitcher's mound. There was a large group of boys standing all around her, holding their new gloves and wearing their favorite team hats and cleats. Their dads were helping and encouraging them. All Emma had was Tom's old Mariners cap and his ragged sneakers. She saw one dad tap his son on the shoulder and point at her. "Don't worry, son. You're better than that kid."

A coach threw her the ball. A batter stepped up to the plate. Emma heard two coaches talking behind her.

"Who's this guy?"

"The Witherspoon kid."

"How is he?"

"Good arm. Flaky, though. Not so good up here," the coach said, and pointed to his head.

Emma ignored them. If there was one thing Emma Baker, activities dork, knew something about, it was focus. She knew how to concentrate. She knew how to zero in on a task and get it done.

She stared hard at home plate. She shook Tom's throwing arm once. It was very strong, if she could control it. She wound up slowly, leaned back, and threw a sizzling fastball. The batter swung wildly, spun around, and almost lost his bat. Strike one.

One coach raised his eyebrows. "Nice pitch," said the other coach.

Emma wound up again and threw a hard curveball, low and outside. The batter reached for it and almost fell over. Strike two.

"Huh."

"Interesting."

"You know, sometimes with these head-case types, if you work with them a little . . ."

Emma wound up and threw a blistering fastball right down the middle. The batter stared in wonder. Strike three.

"I don't see any problems," said the first coach.

"No problems at all," said the second.

"I like the kid."

"I always liked the kid."

"The kid's got poise."

"I want that kid on the A team. First string."

Emma watched the rest of the tryouts from the bench. Various coaches and other players came to congratulate her on her performance. She was used to being the top girl on her gymnastics team, but this was different. For boys, winning was everything. Emma could tell that people were staring at her, envying her, and talking about her. Even the boys' dads were in awe.

Suddenly, she saw Tom come running down the hill. There were still a lot of people hanging around watching the tryouts. Emma watched Tom fight his way through them to the main bulletin board, where the team assignments had just been posted. She could see Tom scanning the list. He looked at the C team first, but he couldn't find his name. He looked at the B team, but he wasn't on that, either. He looked at the A team. He wasn't on that.

She saw a terrified look come over Tom's face and watched him ask one of the coaches a question. The coach pointed to the very top of the board. There was his name: *Tom Witherspoon, #1 A team pitcher.*

Emma smiled when Tom's face lit up. She had never seen him so excited. She walked over and stood behind him. She kind of liked how she towered over him.

"You owe me big-time," Emma whispered.

Tom spun around and hugged her. "Oh my God! Thank you!" he cried. "I'm on A team! I can't believe it! A team!"

"Shhh," Emma said, leading him away from the crowd. "This is all nice and everything. But we kind of need to focus on the arrowhead."

"Of course!" Tom became instantly serious. "What do you think we need to do?"

But just then a voice called out from the school parking lot. "Emma!"

It was Mrs. Baker.

"Shoot!" Emma said. "I forgot. I have Girl Scouts tonight."

"Girl Scouts? Can I skip it?"

"No, we're doing a cookie sale. It's kind of important," she replied.

"All right. I'll call you."

"Sell as fast as you can," Emma said. "We don't have much time!"

As Tom ran across the playground to her mom's car, Emma's head began to fill with worry. They were running out of time. What if this was the Tohaka curse? If they didn't switch back soon, they'd be doomed. And to get stuck selling Girl Scout cookies when the fate of her whole life was at stake? It was amazing how much useless crap she did every day. She had to do something about her schedule when she switched back.

If she switched back.

A SMALL WAGER

Tom had never noticed that the Girl Scouts wore their uniforms to school on their meeting days.

"You never forget to wear this," Mrs. Baker said when he got into the car. She held up a plastic Old Navy bag. "Scoot down and change—no one will see."

He wished. He still couldn't believe he was wearing a Girl Scout uniform: a fitted blue blouse, a short khaki skirt, and a sash. When Mrs. Baker dropped him off outside Safeway, everything seemed to be in its rightful place. More or less.

But when he joined the troop and the girls looked at him as if he were crazy, he discovered that he'd done everything wrong. His sash was on backward. The elastic bracelets he'd put on his wrist were actually headbands. And he had forgotten to change out of his white tube socks with red stripes.

Ashley blinked at him. "Gosh, Emma, you're a mess."

Tom nodded. "I was in a hurry."

"Still," Ashley said, turning his skirt around. "We represent our den and our troop and our district, and our neighborhood, as well as our state, and our country, and really, when you think about it, all Girl Scouts everywhere."

"How about Girl Scouts from other planets?"

"Those too," Ashley said cheerfully. She led him over to a large table that was covered with posters. Boxes of cookies sat on it, and Girl Scouts were busy setting up the cash box and organizing the boxes. "Are we gonna sell some cookies? Are we ready to spread the Girl Scout spirit?" Ashley asked.

Most of them were, at least the ones who weren't looking at Sienna Jones's new lip gloss, "Peachy Keen."

"Okay!" said Ashley. "Let's do it!"

Tom felt ridiculous in his sash, and worst of all, he and Sienna got stuck hitting up customers as they went into the grocery store. They were responsible for selling ten boxes each.

"Wanna buy some cookies?" he asked a gruff-looking man.

The man didn't even answer as he strode into the store.

Guess not, Tom thought.

A woman with a small child in a car seat came up. Tom gave her a big smile. "Good afternoon, ma'am," he said politely. "We're here representing Girl Scouts and apple pie and puppies and stuff, and we've got these cookies and we're kind of in a hurry, so if you wouldn't mind buying a dozen or so—"

"No, thank you," said the woman. The toddler waved as they hurried past.

Then Tom spotted Dustin Fletcher. "Hey, Dustin!" Tom was relieved to see a familiar face. "What's up?"

"Oh, hey," Dustin said. "What are you guys doing here?"

"Selling cookies, bro," Tom said, forgetting himself for the moment. Fortunately, no one noticed.

"Yeah?" Dustin watched as Sienna checked out her appearance in her compact. "What kind are they?"

"Oh. Uh . . . Thin Mints, I think," Tom said. He had not looked at the cookies. "Wanna buy some?"

"I don't like Thin Mints," Dustin said, still staring at Sienna, who was pressing her lips together.

Tom looked over at the boxes. There were tons. He had to start selling some cookies—*now*. "You don't have to like 'em. You just have to buy 'em."

"Hey, Sienna," Dustin said.

"Hello," Sienna answered, without enthusiasm.

"How about we make a little bet?" Tom said, remembering that Dustin always liked to bet on stuff, especially if there were pretty girls around to impress. "I'll bet you can't eat a whole box."

"Why would I want to eat a whole box?" said Dustin. "I don't even like them."

"Okay," said Tom, desperate to make a sale. "I'll bet you *I* can eat a whole box."

Dustin took in Emma's tiny gymnast's body. "You?"

"And I can do it in forty seconds."

"Get out! You can't eat a whole box in forty seconds."

"Wanna bet?"

"Sure, I mean . . . what do you wanna bet?"

"If I can eat a whole box, you gotta buy ten boxes."

"And if you can't?"

"Free cookies for life. Courtesy of the Girl Scouts. And that's not just Thin Mints, that's every kind of cookie." Tom pointed out a few other boxes. "Peanut Butter Patties. Caramel Delites."

"Really? Caramel Delites? And you can do that?"

"Of course. We represent Girl Scouts everywhere. We represent the whole organization."

"Okay. If you swear I can have Caramel Delites. Do you swear?"

"Sure."

"I don't think we have Caramel Delites," Sienna said suddenly.

"Of course we do," Tom insisted.

"Either way," Dustin said. "You gotta swear."

How come Tom had never realized how annoying Dustin could be? He sighed. "I, uh, Emma, swear on my Girl Scout honor that you can have cookies, of any type, for as long as you want, if you win the bet, which you won't, so whatever, so help me God."

"We'll see about that!" Dustin said greedily.

Tom grabbed one of the cookie boxes. Then he remembered: not only did he not have his normal mouth, he didn't have his bottomless pit of a stomach anymore. He had Emma's small mouth and her tiny stomach. This might be harder than he thought.

"All right." Dustin looked at his watch. "Get ready." Tom tore the top off the cookie box. Thankfully, the cookies were divided up in little compartments. There weren't that many of them. Anyway, it wasn't like Tom had a choice. He *had* to get rid of these cookies and *had* to get back to Emma. Time was running out.

"Go!" said Dustin.

Tom crammed the first row of cookies in his mouth. He chewed them as fast as he could. Then he jammed in the next row.

"That's disgusting!" Sienna said, backing away. A few other Girl Scouts took note of what was happening.

"Emma!" Ashley said, sounding horrified. But Tom couldn't stop now. He had to win.

"Nobody that small can eat a whole box in forty seconds," Dustin crowed. He was keeping a close eye on his watch. "You just lost yourself a bet!"

Tom stuffed row after row of cookies in his mouth. As a young boy, he had been a champion speed eater. He had once eaten eleven Hostess cupcakes in sixty seconds. But could Emma's stomach take it?

"Ewww! You're getting chocolate all over your lips," a sickened Girl Scout said. Tom snatched the last of the cookies and scarfed them down. Once they were all crammed into his mouth, he raised his hands in triumph. He'd done it! He'd won! And Emma's stomach and mouth had held up. Maybe girls weren't as lame as he thought.

Dustin shook his head in disbelief. "Wow! Thirty-eight seconds. That's incredible. For a girl."

"Mmmphfffghhhweffmmntr," Tom said while trying to swallow the last of the cookies.

Dustin grudgingly agreed to come back with the money, and Tom handed over the boxes. Then, with a wave to Ashley, he pulled off his sash and raced inside Safeway to call Mrs. Baker. There was no time to lose.

MORNING WOOD

Emma woke up Friday morning feeling more anxious than ever. Tom's sheets smelled so . . . boyish. It reminded her of what a terrible situation she was in. Tom hadn't been able to meet with her after Girl Scouts—he'd been throwing up cookies, or some crazy thing. And of course her mother had hovered over him until after midnight. So they had wasted more precious time. She sat up in bed. They had to get together with the arrowhead. Maybe they could meet before school. She reached for the cell phone on her bedside table. . . .

That was when she saw it. It was some sort of creature, a mouse or a bird or a chipmunk. It was under the covers and its head stuck straight up, forming a little tent where her lap was.

Emma did not do well with wild animals, especially

small rodent-sized ones. She tried to scoot out of the bed, slowly. But when she moved, it suddenly moved too. "Ahhhh!" she cried.

Right after she screamed, she heard someone running down the hall. It was Ricky. He tried opening her door, but it was locked.

"What's wrong?" Ricky shouted from the other side of the door.

"There's something in my bed! A chipmunk or something!"

"I'll get my bear trap!" yelled Ricky before thumping down the hall again.

Terrified, Emma continued to study the lump in her bed. But she also noticed an odd feeling near her waist. Her boy thing felt funny. Maybe the creature was sitting right on top of it. Maybe it had built a nest!

There was only one thing to do: lift the blankets and shoo it away. She gripped the top of her blankets and pulled them up slowly. She expected it to come scurrying out and attack her. But nothing happened. She lifted the blankets higher, and then the sheet, until she could see. What was it? What was down there? It was . . . oh my God . . . could it be . . . ?

Emma had a *boner*.

A minute later, Ricky pounded on the door. "I have my bear trap," he yelled. "And my tennis racket. I'll bash it on the head! Open up!"

Emma yanked the sheet back down. She stared at the spot where her blankets were sticking straight up. *So that's why they call it pitching a tent*, she thought.

"Let me in!" Ricky yelled.

"Never mind!" Emma called. "It's gone. I think it ran away."

"What's going on?" said a grown-up voice. It was Tom's mother.

"Nothing!" Emma shouted. She wanted to push the blanket down but she was afraid to touch it. Ms. Andre had told the class *why* boys got them and *how* boys got them, but she'd never said how to make them go away.

"Tom, honey, what's the matter?" Tom's mother asked. "Are you okay?"

"Uh . . ." Emma tried to think. Brad talked about erections all the time, but she rarely listened because he was a walking gross-out factory. But she did remember one thing he'd said: *to get rid of one, you have to think of something embarrassing.*

That was it. Emma tried to think of something embarrassing. But what was more embarrassing than what was happening right now?

Ricky pounded on the door with his tennis racket. "Let! Me! In!" he demanded.

"Tom, open the door," Mrs. Witherspoon said.

Emma was doing everything she could to make it go away. She was standing up now. She tried pushing it down. To the side. But no matter what she did, it popped back out. She scrambled for the cell phone and punched in her number. He answered on the fourth ring.

"Tom!" she whispered. "Oh my God. You have to help me. I have one!"

"One what?" Tom asked.

"You know. A whatchamacallit!"

Tom yawned. "What's a whatchamacallit?"

"You know, one of *those*. What Ms. Andre told us about!"

"You're having a baby?"

"No! I'm having a . . . thingy."

"I don't know what a thingy is."

Silence. "A *boner*. A tent pole. A stiff willy."

"Really?" Tom said. This news seemed to wake him up. "Wow. How'd you do that? Were you thinking about Kelly Angstrom?"

Emma slapped at it again as if it were a naughty child. "No, dork. I woke up with it!"

"Welcome to my world," Tom said through a yawn.

"But your brother and your mom are right outside my door! What do I do? How do I get rid of it?"

More silence. "Well, there's one way that definitely works."

"Eww! I'm not doing *that*. I'm not *touching* it."

"Okay, then try thinking of something painful. Imagine some kung fu dude kicking you right in the nu—"

"I don't have time to imagine some kung fu dude!"

"Okay, then imagine you're on a dirt bike. And you totally bite it and the handlebars go straight into your ba—"

"Oh no!" said Emma. Ricky had slipped a screwdriver into the lock of her door and was twisting it open. Emma had just managed to slip the phone under the covers of her bed when the door swung open. Tom's mother stood in the doorway. Ricky was trying to see around her. He wore

115

Tom's football helmet and was holding a tennis racket, ready to attack.

Mrs. Witherspoon saw what the problem was. She quickly pushed Ricky back and came into the room.

"Aww, come on!" whined Ricky from the hallway. "I wanna whack it! What if it gets away?"

"This is not something you whack," Mrs. Witherspoon said, closing the door behind her. She turned to Emma, flustered. "Now, Tom . . . I know it must be a shock to wake up with . . . *that thing*. But it happens to all boys your age. It's called an erection."

"Mm-hmm," said Emma, who was now bright red. "I know."

"And it's nothing to worry about. It's perfectly normal."

Thankfully, the embarrassment of talking to Tom's mom was doing exactly what Tom had predicted. It was going down.

Mrs. Witherspoon looked wistful. "I wish I could help you more with these kinds of things. Dad would—"

"Don't worry, Mom," Emma said, feeling bad for her. "We talked about it in health class."

"I know you did. But—"

"Mom, don't get down on yourself. Just because Dad isn't here doesn't mean we're not still a family."

"You're right," Tom's mom said quietly. "You're absolutely right. Thank you for saying that."

"Sure," Emma said, and gave her a hug. Mrs. Witherspoon looked shocked. Emma supposed Tom wasn't the touchy-feely type. So she gave her another for good measure.

116

"Thanks, honey," Mrs. Witherspoon said, touching Emma's cheek.

"You're welcome."

"You seem so much older lately. And more mature. You're growing up or something."

"Or something," Emma said, and smiled.

RUMORS SPREAD

Tom arrived at school after a particularly frustrating morning with Claire. She had criticized everything he had put on, right down to his socks. Now he was sweating with nerves. Would Emma even make it to first period? Being the opposite sex was turning into a full-time job. Whenever either of them had a moment to themselves, some new problem popped up. Literally.

And a new problem was just what was waiting for Tom at school. As soon as he got there, he noticed several sixth-grade girls looking at him funny. Then some eighth-grade boys saw him and began whispering.

Then, in the girls' bathroom, two seventh graders came up to him.

"Is it true?" the first girl asked.

"Is what true?"

Could they know he was a boy inside Emma's body?

"You know what," said the second girl.

Tom tried to stay cool. "No, I don't."

The girl's eyes narrowed. "So you deny it?"

"Deny what?"

The girl could hardly contain herself. "That you were in the janitor's closet on Wednesday? With Tom Witherspoon?"

Tom had forgotten about the closet incident. To him it seemed like a million years ago. But of course, it was really only a day and a half. And now the rumors had spread to the seventh grade. By lunchtime the whole school would know.

"Nothing happened," Tom said. His stomach felt all twisty. "We were just talking."

"Yeah, right!" said the seventh graders. Several of the others scowled at him with disapproval. Then the bell rang and Tom was off the hook. For now.

After second period, Tom and Emma finally got a chance to talk in the back of the library. They had to figure out what to do with the arrowhead.

"I say we sneak back into the gym and get back on the trampoline," Tom whispered. "And then we'll bounce around and bash heads, just like we did before."

"But they already packed the trampoline away," Emma said, her head in her hands. Well, *his* hands.

"We'll get it out again. We'll sneak into the storage area. . . ."

"But what if the curse isn't about that?" Emma said. "I think it's more about understanding. That's what it said

119

on the Web site. Maybe we need to go somewhere and be alone and really figure some stuff out. Like why we always fight."

"We always fight because that's what boys and girls do," Tom said.

"But why?"

"Who knows? Why is the sky blue? Why is the ocean full of water? And how do we know this Winnihecket guy even cares? What if he's asleep?"

Emma frowned. "That is so typical of you. Just assuming that everyone is as lazy as you."

"What else am I supposed to think? I don't even know if I believe this whole curse thing. Maybe it's something else. Maybe this is a reality show. Maybe we're on *Punk'd* right now!"

"The curse makes perfect sense," Emma insisted. "And we fit the profile exactly. We're just like those people."

"Those people were married!" Tom said. "They lived in the ice fields. We're in sixth grade!"

"So what? Back in ancient times people younger than us got married."

"Lucky them!"

"Listen," Emma said. "We built that tree house together. We were practically best friends. Now we argue all the time and we're mean to each other. We never try to see things from the other person's point of view, which is exactly what happened to the cursed couple."

Tom shook his head, but he knew she was right. "So what do we have to do?"

"We have to show the Winnihecket guy we can cooperate and respect each other."

"And how do we do that?"

"If we go somewhere by ourselves and really talk to each other, talk about everything we don't like about the other person, every reason we've ever argued . . . if we can get it all out, really clear the air, really get in touch with our feelings—"

"But I hate getting in touch with my feelings!" Tom groaned.

"Do you have any better ideas?"

Tom didn't. He shook his head.

"So will you try this?" Emma asked. "And be totally open and honest?"

Tom shrugged. "I dunno. I can try."

"Then let's do it," said Emma. "I'll meet you after school. We'll talk about everything. I think it will work. I really do."

Tom nodded reluctantly.

"Now get to class. People don't expect me to be late."

Tom did as he was told and ran to his locker. That was when he noticed several girls and boys giggling and staring at him. The same seventh grader who had confronted him in the bathroom shot him an evil look.

Now what's going on? Tom thought.

When he got to Emma's locker, he found out. Someone had written a message down the length of it in felt pen:

Dear Kissy Face,
    Meet me in the janitor's
closet. I wanna make
out some more!
Your big stud, Tom

Tom couldn't believe it. Everyone around him was laughing. He'd never felt so tiny and defenseless in his life.

"Hey, Emma, what's it like being Tom Witherspoon's gal pal?" said a passing fifth grader. Tom was so upset and humiliated that, without thinking, he grabbed the boy by the collar and rammed his head into the lockers.

"Ouch!" said the boy. He looked at Tom like he was crazy.

"I did not kiss Tom Witherspoon! Do you understand?" Everyone in the hall stared at him. He was not acting like Emma, or any girl.

Tom tried to simmer down. He let go of the shaking fifth grader. "I—I mean . . . ," he stammered. "I'm really going to be upset . . . if I get in trouble for this writing on my locker."

But the damage was done.

"What is *up* with you?" Courtney said as she pushed through the crowd. "First you don't even tell us about Tom and the janitor's closet. And now you're beating up defenseless fifth graders? The whole point of Grrlzillas is we're supposed to stick together."

Tom stared at Courtney and the others. He had no idea what to say or how to respond. Then he remembered Emma telling him if things ever got really bad he could always cry and run to the nearest bathroom. It was a girl's natural right. So Tom took a deep breath, closed his eyes, did his best girl-crying imitation, and dashed to the bathroom.

Unfortunately, the girls just followed him in there. When he went into a stall, they lined up outside it and continued their verbal assault.

"I'm going to the bathroom, do you mind?" he said.

The girls didn't care. Courtney stood just outside the stall door. "Emma, the Grrlzillas are very disappointed in you!"

Oh, gimme a break, thought Tom.

"If you say you didn't do anything in that janitor's closet, we believe you. But you have to talk to us about it."

"I can't. I'm going to the bathroom," said Tom. And to prove it, he pulled down his purple low-riders and sat on the toilet.

"We want to believe you, but you're not telling us things. We need to know why and we need to know *now!*"

Tom tried to think of a girl-like excuse. "I just have a lot going on."

"Then tell us about it!" Courtney said.

"I'm having a bad hair day," Tom said.

"We have bad hair days too!" a few of the girls said in unison.

"And I don't feel good about myself," Tom said.

"We can help you with that. But not if you avoid us and don't tell us what's wrong. We mean it, Emma. Come out and talk to us. Please," Courtney begged.

Why wouldn't they leave him alone? Tom tried to think

of a better excuse. "I'm just having . . . ," he began. What could he tell them? How could he get out of this?

That was when he saw something in his striped panties. It was a little dark spot. He looked closer. . . .

"Well?" demanded Courtney. "What are you having?"

He gulped hard. *"My first period?"*

EMMA MISSES A VERY IMPORTANT MOMENT

Emma was in study hall writing down everything she didn't like about Tom, sixth-grade boys in particular, and all boys in general. She wanted to have all her complaints ready for her open and honest discussion with Tom. The real challenge would be getting Tom to come clean.

Then her cell phone vibrated in her pocket. Luckily the study hall teacher was way too busy using her Blackberry to actually watch the class. Emma snuck out to the hall and answered it.

"Hey, Emma, it's Tom."

"I'm in study hall, I can't talk. What is it?"

"Well, it kind of is . . . I need to ask you . . . have you ever . . . you know . . . had your . . . monthly . . . girl thing?"

"My period? That's none of your business."

"It is now."

"What? Did you have it? That's impossible."

"Apparently it is possible."

"Shut up!" Emma shouted. "It can't be!"

"Shhhhhh," said Tom. "Calm down."

"Calm down? Are you serious? You had my first period! What did you do that for? *I'm* supposed to have my first period! Not you!"

"No kidding!" Tom whispered.

Emma was extremely upset. "This can't be happening. A *boy* had my first period. Okay. Don't panic. Breathe." She tried to calm down. She looked up and down the hallway to make sure no one could hear her. "All right, tell me from the beginning. Tell me *exactly* what happened."

"Uh," Tom said. "Well, I was sitting in the stall. I looked down and I saw a spot on my underwear, so I told Courtney. Then everyone got very excited and they all squeezed into the stall and showed me what to do."

"They showed you? *They showed you?* Oh my God, I can't believe I missed this!"

"It was sort of cool," Tom admitted. "The way everyone helped out. In fact, Courtney let me borrow her cell so I could call my mother—I mean, your mother. That's how I was able to call you. I didn't know girls could be so nice to each other."

"Of course they're nice during *that!*"

"Then they got Ms. Andre," Tom said. "They brought her into the bathroom to talk to me."

"Ms. Andre came *into* the bathroom? And *talked* to you? What did she say?"

"The same stuff she says in health class. You know, once a month . . . a special moment . . . part of becoming a woman . . . all that."

"She said it was a *special moment*? Oh my God. I can't believe I missed my first period. I'm going to have a panic attack!"

"I don't see why you're so freaked out," Tom said. "It'll happen again. That's what Ms. Andre said—just wait a month. I just hope it happens to you next time."

Emma tried to hold back her tears. "It's one of the biggest milestones in a girl's life. And I *missed* it."

"Well, I've still got the underpants, you know, if you want to save the memory."

After school, Emma sulked as she walked down to the baseball field. It was the first A team practice. The other boys were playing catch. Emma, still stunned that she'd missed a major moment in her life, kicked at the dirt on the field and threw her glove into the back-stop.

Suddenly, Kelly Angstrom appeared. "Hey, Tom," she said with a big smile. "Congratulations on making number one pitcher."

Emma nodded bashfully.

"I always knew you would," Kelly purred. "It's really cool that you're becoming such a star athlete." Then she handed Emma an envelope. "I'm having a party on Saturday. I hope you can come."

Kelly skipped away. Emma opened the envelope and read the invitation:

Come Celebrate Kelly Angstrom's Thirteenth Birthday!
Yeah, that's right! I'm a teenager!
This Saturday
5:00 p.m. pizza
5:30 p.m. cake and presents
6:00 p.m. to 8:00 p.m. movie in basement:
Teenage Fantasy Princess 5!
RSVP to Kelly's mom, and don't be late!

Emma felt her spirits rising. She'd been invited to birthday parties before, but never by someone as popular as Kelly Angstrom. It made her feel good to be in demand. Of course, she couldn't go. She had body-switching stuff to do. But it was nice to feel wanted.

Then Jeff Matthews came strutting by. "I see you got the invite," he said.

"Yeah," Emma murmured. Although she had lost some of her faith in Jeff, he was still extremely hot.

"You know what happens during the movie, don't ya?" asked Jeff.

"No. What?"

"Dawg, that's when the kissing action starts."

"Kissing action?"

"Bro, you think Kelly Angstrom is going to have a party without kissing games? All this pizza and crap, that's for the parents. The basement movie—that's when the *real* party is."

Emma's entire body went numb. Kissing games? She found herself slightly intrigued by the idea. Or she would have been, if she hadn't been in Tom Witherspoon's body.

Jeff smacked Emma in the back of the head so her baseball cap fell off. "Dude, you look like you've never made out with someone before. Which we know isn't true, *Mr. Janitor*."

"Oh." Emma sighed. "Yeah."

"Hey, maybe *I* can get with that Emma girl this time. You wouldn't have a problem with that, would you? I mean, it's not like you guys are going out."

"No. I mean, yes, I mean, I don't—"

"Jeez, dude, get a grip." Jeff whacked Emma in the head again. "I'm just kidding. I would never hit on Emma Baker. She's way too straight for me."

"Yeah, right," Emma mumbled.

TOM VS. GRRLZILLAS

Tom was having his own troubles at after-school gymnastics. After she'd calmed down, Emma had explained to him the basics of the routine she was supposed to perform at Saturday's meet. Much to Tom's surprise, with his small, athletic body, he could actually do most of it. The other surprise: Gymnastics was sort of fun, even if he was wearing a maxi-pad.

The only problem was the other girls. They wouldn't talk to him. Tom couldn't figure out what the deal was. They wouldn't look at him or even go near him.

After everyone was finished stretching, Rachel Simms finally broke the silence. Tom was trying to do a back extension roll when she approached him. "What's the problem? That move looks awful."

"I'll get it," said Tom. "I'm just a little rusty is all."

"Maybe if you spent more time in here and less time in the *boys'* locker room . . ."

"I told you before," he said. "Nothing happened with Tom."

"Yeah, right," said Rachel. "Like everyone in school doesn't know about you guys." She stomped back to where the other girls were.

Ashley tried to be nice, though. When she'd finished her own routine, she tiptoed over to Tom and said, "They're just jealous because something exciting happened to you."

Tom could make some sense out of that. Brad had been jealous about his pitching skills, but still, he'd never been mean. Girls were tough, tougher than boys in some ways. No wonder Emma stuck to her schoolwork. It was safer.

A tall girl with freckles did a few backflips, and when she landed, she whispered, "Oh, look, it's the Make-Out Queen."

"Say it again," Tom whispered back, "and I'll flip you right out the window!"

That shut the girls up for a while, but it made for a silent practice. Tom was glad when it was over. Outside the gym, he called Emma.

"I just got home from baseball practice," Emma said. "I wrote down some things we can talk about. You better do the same."

Tom wasn't much for writing stuff down, but he promised to think about it. "Where should we meet?"

"At the tree house," she said. "But first I have to go get the arrowhead."

Tom gasped. "You don't have it with you? Where is it?"

131

"Um . . . at your house," said Emma.

Tom was so upset, his whole body began to tremble. "At my house?"

"Well, it wasn't safe to bring it to school. Your spastic friends almost broke it!"

"But you shouldn't have left it at my house. Ricky will get it!"

"No, he won't. I stashed it. It's safe."

"Are you nuts? Ricky can find *anything*. And the more you don't want him to find something, the faster he finds it!" Tom shouted.

"I'm not an idiot, Tom. Ricky's seven years old and I already tricked him once. Don't be so paranoid."

Now he was sweating heavily. "I'm not being paranoid! This is a *little brother* we're talking about, which you have obviously never had."

"I promise you. There's no way. I hid it under the mattress of your bed. What are the odds he'll look there?"

"Under the mattress? That's where boys stash everything!" Tom shook his head. There were just some things a girl would never understand.

MISSION IMPROBABLE

Emma was sure Ricky wouldn't find the arrowhead. But there was something in Tom's voice that worried her. Could Ricky really be that nosy? Later that afternoon, Emma went to the Witherspoon house and ran into Tom's room. She pushed the desk chair out of the way and lifted up the mattress. She didn't see the arrowhead. She lifted the mattress higher. A Victoria's Secret catalog was the only thing there. The arrowhead had disappeared.

Tom had been right.

Emma bolted down the hall and burst into Tom's mother's room. Mrs. Witherspoon was sitting on the bed, folding laundry and watching the evening news.

"Mom," Emma said, breathing hard. "Where's Ricky?"

Mrs. Witherspoon didn't look up. "He's staying over at

William's house tonight, honey. Why? What did he do this time?"

"He took something. Something that I need. Very badly."

"Can you get it later? They went to the movies." Mrs. Witherspoon checked her clock radio. "They left at five. They're long gone by now."

Emma couldn't believe her ears. She would have to call Tom and explain that he was right. And she had . . . lost the arrowhead. Or had she? After all, she was Emma Baker, problem solver. She'd outsmarted Ricky once. Maybe she could do it again.

She went to Tom's room and dug through his desk for possible tools and supplies. She found a flashlight, binoculars, and a black hat. She also grabbed the big fake plastic eyeball that Tom had had in his cargo pants. *That's a start,* she thought.

At seven-forty-five William's mom's car pulled into the driveway of their house. Emma turned off the lights and watched through the binoculars. Ricky and William did not go inside. Instead, they headed for the garage.

Emma slipped out the back door. It was a warm spring night. She felt the thrill of the hunt as she crossed the street and darted silently across the neighbors' lawn. She crept up to William's garage and pressed herself against the outside wall. Inside, she could hear Ricky and William talking. Staying hidden in the shadows, she snuck a peek to see what they were doing.

They were hitting things with a hammer. Ricky was wearing Tom's football helmet and they were staring at whatever it was they had just flattened into oblivion.

Then Ricky pulled something out of his pocket. "Look what I brought!"

William took the item in his hands. "Your brother's arrowhead. Does he know you got it?"

"It's not his. I found it in a secret cave!"

"No, you didn't. You found it under his mattress. I was there."

"No way!" said Ricky, who always had a story for everything. "And it's not an arrowhead. It's a secret grenade that blows things up!"

William touched it and admired its smooth surface.

"I'm going to stick it right here," Ricky said. He grabbed it from William and jammed it into the face guard of the football helmet.

"But I thought it was a grenade."

"No," Ricky said. "It's not. It's a secret badge that means I'm a spy."

"But I thought we were samurai," said William.

"Let's go blow something up!"

"We can't. You heard my mom. We're not allowed to leave the garage."

As the two boys argued, Emma came up with a plan. She dug the fake eyeball out of her pocket, then leaned forward and rolled it just inside the garage, so that it came to rest beside William.

So far, so good, she thought.

Within seconds, Ricky spotted the large white eye next to William. "Wow, look! An eyeball!"

"Whoooaa!" said William.

Ricky grabbed it before his friend could and tried to smash it with his hammer. However, when he hit it, the eyeball shot across the garage floor.

William ran after it. "That's not how you smash an eyeball!" He tried to smash it with his foot, but it rolled under the car and into the driveway. William picked up a baseball bat and tried to smash it with that.

"Wait!" Ricky said suddenly. "Let's put it in the vise!"

"Yeah, maybe it'll squish!"

"Maybe it'll pop!"

"Hey, wait a minute," William said. "Where did it come from?"

They both stopped and thought for a moment. "Maybe it was planted here by ninjas!" Ricky said.

"Maybe it's a spy eyeball and it's looking at us!"

"Do you think it can see us right now?"

William shrugged. "Probably. It's an eyeball."

"It must be ninjas!" cried Ricky. "It must be a sneak attack!"

"What do we do?" William asked.

"We attack back!"

Emma ducked behind the wall. The next thing she saw was Ricky running down the driveway swinging a golf club and throwing golf balls in every direction.

"*Bcchhew! Bchew! Kabloooom!*" Ricky loved making his own sound effects.

Emma watched this from behind the garbage cans. The arrowhead was still lodged in the face mask of Tom's football helmet. She had to get it . . . and fast.

136

Then William's father appeared at the door. "What's going on out here?" he said sharply. He looked more closely at Ricky. "Are those *my* new golf clubs?"

A few minutes later the playdate was over and Ricky was escorted home. Emma watched as Ricky and Mrs. Witherspoon talked in the doorway. Suddenly Ricky tore off Tom's helmet and threw it down the driveway, where it rolled all the way to the street. It sat there beside the curb, rocking from side to side. Good move for Emma. Bad move for Ricky. Mrs. Witherspoon did not look happy. Ricky would be paying for that one.

Emma appeared from behind a parked car and scooped the helmet up. The arrowhead was still in one piece.

Mission accomplished, she thought. *Now on to meet Tom.*

But before Emma could make her escape, Mrs. Witherspoon spotted her in the street. "Tom? Is that you?" she called out. "I want you inside too."

"But Mom," Emma whined. "I'm just going for a walk."

"A walk?" Mrs. Witherspoon shook her head. "Inside. And no complaining."

Emma trudged into the house. She'd just have to hope they could make the arrowhead work tomorrow. If not, they'd be out of time—and out of luck.

DREAMS OF KISSING KELLY

Tom's eyes snapped open the second the phone rang beside him. He'd stayed up for hours the night before, waiting for Emma to call him, but she never had. That definitely wasn't a good sign. Tom was praying that this was her now.

"Hello," he mumbled.

"Emma? It's me, Ashley."

Tom's heart sank. "Oh, hi."

"I just wanted to tell you before I left for soccer practice that I think it's entirely unfair that the other girls are being mean to you and not believing your story about Tom Witherspoon."

Tom looked at his clock. It was eight-fifteen. Wasn't it too early on a Saturday to be talking about stuff like this? Not for girls, Tom supposed. "Thanks."

"I also want to invite you to Kelly's birthday party tonight. Kelly was going to ask you, but some of the other girls talked her out of it. I really think you should go. Show 'em you're tough, like you did at practice."

Tom sat up. Kelly was having a party? This was interesting news. "So it's tonight?"

"Yes. A lot of boys will be there. And we're gonna play kissing games too. At least, that's what people are saying."

"Kissing games?"

"That's right. Oops, I have to go. Hope to see you later."

"Thanks," Tom said, and hung up.

He got up, stretched his arms, and looked around the room, only to see that Mrs. Baker had laid out Emma's gymnastics leotard for him last night. She'd even placed the pixie slippers neatly together on the floor.

Oh no, he thought. *The gymnastics meet.* He had done pretty well at practice—he'd pretty much passed as Emma. But could he handle a major competition? Tom's cell rang again. Thankfully, it was Emma.

"Tom? I got the arrowhead back!"

"Well, if you'd listened to me you'd never have lost it."

"Don't argue. This is the last day. We have to meet."

"I would," Tom whispered. "The only problem is I have another Emma Baker activity this morning. I have that dumb gymnastics meet."

"Can you get out of it?" she asked.

"What do you think? Did you ever get out of anything when you were yourself?"

Emma huffed. "No, I guess not."

"I also just found out Kelly Angstrom's having a party tonight," Tom said.

"Oh yeah, you got invited to that," Emma replied.

"I did? Who invited me?"

"Kelly, obviously. It's her party."

"Kelly invited me," Tom marveled. Then he frowned. "And you weren't going to tell me about it?"

"Why would I tell you? We can't go."

"Maybe *you* can't go," Tom insisted. "But *I'm* sure as heck going. A kissing party? With Kelly Angstrom? I'm not missing that. No way. Not for anything."

"Tom. Idiot. You're *me*. You can't kiss Kelly Angstrom, even if you're there."

Tom had to think about that for a second.

"If we go to that party, I'm the one who'll have to kiss her," Emma continued. "And trust me, the last thing in the world I want is to kiss anyone. Not in your body."

"But I can't miss a chance to kiss Kelly Angstrom. She's not going to like me forever."

"I would hope not."

"So we'll just have to switch back before the party," Tom said enthusiastically. "Have you figured out what we need to do?"

But just as Emma was about to answer, Mrs. Baker came in. "You're not dressed yet?" she asked Tom. "You better hurry up. You're supposed to be there in an hour."

When Emma's mom left the room, Tom said into the phone, "I'll see you at the tree house after the meet. All right?"

"Okay, but Tom?"

"Yeah?"

"Can you try to get me a decent score?"

After what she had done for him in baseball, it was the least he could do. "I'll try. But to tell you the truth, I wasn't so great in practice. I'm not as good as you."

"Well, at least make it seem like you know what you're doing," Emma said with a sigh.

But two hours later, as Tom stood at the corner of the gymnastics mat, he wasn't sure he knew anything. The crowd in the middle school gym was filled with judges, parents, coaches, and students. Tom got nervous looking around the room, and it didn't help that he was dressed in a wedgie-inducing black leotard and pixie slippers.

"Next up," boomed a deep voice over the loudspeaker, "Emma Baker, with her first floor exercise."

Tom stepped onto the mat. The crowd went silent. He swallowed.

Emma had shown him her ritual. She always chalked her hands. She wiggled her shoulders to make sure she was loose. And she always had a "silent moment" when she closed her eyes and emptied her mind, just before she began.

Tom tried to do the same. He poured some chalk into his hands, but when he clapped his palms together, a huge cloud of white powder exploded in front of him. It made him cough. Then the white dust got in his eyes and hair. Not good.

From the side he heard Mrs. Weissman say, "Emma, focus. And where's that big smile?"

"Right," Tom said. Emma had told him to smile no matter what.

Tom pasted a ridiculous grin across his face. He stood at the corner of the mat and shook his shoulders. He closed his eyes and tried to empty his mind, but he couldn't. His brain had one very big thought in it that repeated itself over and over: *You are about to make a total fool of yourself.* He gave up on concentrating and opened his eyes. Everyone was staring at him. One of the other girls waved him forward. "What are you waiting for?" she whispered. "Go!"

Here goes nothing, Tom thought.

He ran hard across the mat, took a skip step, and did a cartwheel, a back handspring, and a back roll and bounced onto his feet. The audience cheered and clapped. Tom breathed a huge sigh of relief. Emma's body was so limber! If he didn't psych himself out, maybe he could get through the routine in one piece.

Tom did two more tumbling passes and then continued into the dance routine that came next. As the Jackson Five's "Dancing Machine" played over the loudspeaker, Tom pointed his toes and pranced around like a flower in the wind or whatever he was supposed to be. That was when he caught sight of Jeff Matthews, who was drinking a Mountain Dew and staring at him with an arrogant smirk.

Tom kept going, turning gracefully to the side, but the sight of Jeff made him forget his dance routine. Then realizing he was forgetting made him *totally* forget. It was the same problem he had in baseball. When the pressure was on, his mind began to wander. He did a half turn and found himself standing with his arms up, one leg pointed to the side, without a clue as to what came next.

"Big smile!" Mrs. Weissman stage-whispered.

Tom bailed on the dance stuff and ran down the mat again, smiling so wide his mouth hurt. His ending was a cartwheel, a handspring, and then what? He managed the cartwheel, lost control of the handspring, and went flying into the crowd. He crashed into a fifth grader, bounced off some grown-ups, knocked a judge off her chair, and rolled until he stopped against two strong legs. He looked up into the eyes of Jeff.

"You're not doing so good, Toadstool," Jeff said between sips of his soda. "But that's okay. I hear you're better in the janitor's closet."

Tom was about to punch Jeff in the face, but when he tried to plant his feet, he felt a sharp pain in his ankle. Mrs. Weissman and the other girls from the team surrounded him.

"Don't move!" one of the girls cried. "Your ankle might be broken!"

Mrs. Weissman shook her head and gave him a sad look. "We're going to need a stretcher."

For now, Tom's humiliation was over, but in a few hours, if he didn't meet up with Emma, this pain would only be the beginning.

A CHANCE OF SHOWERS

Emma sat in the tree fort, waiting for Tom. Valuable time was being wasted. This was day four—their absolute last chance to reverse the curse. She was so anxious, she thought she might throw up. Unfortunately, minutes turned into an hour and Tom still hadn't arrived. The gymnastics meet should have been over an hour before. After another half hour, she had to pee, but she didn't dare leave because he might show up at any minute. She lay down on the old carpet and shut her eyes. *C'mon, Tom, we're running out of time.*

Then there was a loud noise. Emma sat up. A gang of eighth-grade boys was walking past, and one of them had thrown something at the tree house.

"Wait!" said the boy. "Did you see that? Someone's up there."

Emma tried to duck, but it was too late.

"Sweet. Let's nail him!"

All the boys picked up dirt clods. They began target practice on Emma and the tree house. Emma threw herself on the floor as dirt clods exploded all around her.

When the surprise dirt-clod attack stopped, she looked down. She recognized one of her assailants—Bryce Edwards, who was on the track team.

"Hey, look," Bryce yelled. "It's Witherspoon!"

Emma was relieved that they recognized her, so she stood up and waved. "Hey, guys. What's up?"

But none of them answered. Instead, they all picked up more dirt clods. One of them grabbed a large stick. Another got a hold of a rotten apple. "Hey!" she screamed while ducking. An apple burst just above her head and showered her with rotten apple bits. "What are you doing? It's me, Tom. Tom, your friend?"

"Tom the sixth grader, you mean," said one of the eighth graders. "And you know what we do to sixth graders."

"Wedgies!"

"Deluxe wedgies!"

"Ultrawedgies!"

"But you guys," Emma pleaded. "Is that really necessary?"

"Sure. Sixth graders *need* wedgies," said one boy. "It helps your emotional development."

"Triple deluxe wedgies for all sixth graders!" Bryce cried.

"But you guys already got me in trouble," Emma whimpered. "You practically ruined Emma Baker's life with all the rumors, and now you've trashed my fort. Isn't that enough?"

They all looked at each other and smiled. "No," they answered.

"Nothing's the same as a wedgie," said one of them. "It does a body good."

"A sixth grader without a wedgie . . . it's not right," Bryce added. "It's not natural."

What was she going to do now? She was trapped. She had to go to the bathroom badly. And she was going to get a triple deluxe wedgie, which didn't sound very pleasant. They would probably hang her on a tree branch or something. What if she fell? What if she peed her pants?

The boys were gathering at the base of the tree, deciding who should go first. What could Emma do? Desperate, she tried throwing the bits of dirt and rotten apples down at them. Lame! Then she thought of Tom. How would he get out of this? She squeezed her eyes shut and concentrated on everything she had learned about boys.

There was only one solution. She got up off the floor and walked to the opening in the wooden planks above where the eighth graders were gathered.

She undid her belt.

She unzipped her pants.

She set her feet.

She took aim.

"What the—" cried one of the eighth graders. They all looked up.

"Whoa!"

"No way!"

"*Run!*"

The eighth graders sprinted away with the speed of Olympians. Emma had never seen humans move so fast. *Wow*, she thought. Such was the power of the boy position.

And she hadn't even peed.

FRENCH KISSING

While Emma was fighting off her attackers, Tom was at the hospital. His ankle was sprained, but the sprain wasn't bad—if he'd been a boy, he would have just limped home and iced it. But he was Emma now, and Mrs. Baker took every precaution.

After several hours of wrappings and aspirin and nurses and doctors, Emma's mother went to fill out some paperwork. Tom headed for a pay phone.

"Emma!" Tom said when she answered the cell. "Where are you?"

"Where am I?" she said. "Where the heck are you? I waited in the tree house for hours!"

"I'm in the hospital," he said. "I sprained my ankle. Um, I mean, your ankle."

"How did you do that?"

"I fell, genius. Doing your dumb gymnastics routine."

"How did you do? Did you win?"

"Did I win?" Tom repeated. "Would I be sitting in the hospital if I won?"

"Did the team lose?"

"Emma, who cares? I'm in the hospital and I'm still a frickin' girl!"

"Well, what are we gonna do?"

"Your mom is finishing up with the receptionist," Tom said. "Can we meet in the tree house?"

"I don't think we better."

"Why not?"

"Some eighth graders came by. They might come back."

Tom sighed. "We can't go to your house. Your mother will be hovering around."

"I know, and we better not come here. Ricky will spy on us."

"Maybe we should go to Kelly's place," Tom said.

"To her birthday party?"

"Yeah, at least we'll have a chance to be alone."

"Maybe you're right," Emma said. "And it's almost five anyway. Okay. I'll see you there."

Tom arrived at Kelly's party first. People were nice to him, since he was on crutches, but he was only Emma Baker, not one of the "hot" people, so he quickly became just another guest sitting around the table eating pizza. Rachel and Hannah were sitting beside him, whispering excitedly.

"So when do we kiss the boys?" Rachel asked.

"I don't know," Hannah answered. "Whenever they're done playing Xbox in the living room."

"I wonder what kissing tastes like."

"Sienna says it tastes like milk," Hannah said. "But I don't see how it could. Unless the guy just drank some. It probably tastes like spit. That's what's in there."

"Yeah, but what does spit taste like?"

"Watery, and sort of . . . like your mouth, I guess," said Hannah.

Tom tried to stay out of this odd conversation. He didn't want to remind people of the janitor's-closet controversy. He reached for some Pepsi and scooted away from the girls.

But the boys were having kissing conversations too.

"So how does this game actually work?" Zach asked Brad.

"You draw names. And whoever you get, that's who you kiss."

"That seems kind of easy."

"It is easy. That's the thing. The girls actually want to do it."

"Why, though? None of these girls like us."

"Yeah, but they still want to kiss boys. So they don't feel like dorks when they get to high school."

"That's kind of a sweet deal for us."

"It sure is," said Brad.

The doorbell rang again. It was Emma, dressed up in her best Tom outfit—his old Mariners hat, his cargo pants, and his favorite red shirt. Courtney and several of the other girls blushed and acted nervous. *Wow*, thought Tom. *Girls are really starting to like me.*

Tom tried to catch Emma's eye, but there were too many people around. He ate his pizza and listened to Rachel and Ashley, who were still discussing the finer points of kissing.

"You sort of turn your head and close your eyes," Rachel mumbled. "Then you put your lips out."

"*I'm* not closing my eyes," Ashley said.

"Why not?"

"*What if they try something?*"

"You *want* them to try something," said Rachel. "That's what's supposed to happen."

Tom drank his Pepsi and leaned in to eavesdrop on Brad and Zach's discussion.

"So, dude," said Zach. "What's the French-kissing thing?"

"That's when you stick your tongue in their mouth," Brad said.

"Really? And they like it?"

"I guess so."

"Do you have to ask 'em first?"

"Nah, you just do it," Brad said. "They think it's romantic and French and stuff."

"And after you stick it in there, then what?"

"You swish it around."

"Sounds kinda gross," said Zach. "What about your hands? Where do you put them?"

"Around their waist," Brad replied. Then he lowered his voice: "Unless you wanna try for the classic one-hand release."

"What's that?" Zach whispered.

"It's a top-secret bra-release technique."

"Really? How's it work?"

While Brad explained the maneuver, Tom ate pizza and watched Kelly, who was spilling out of her shirt even more than usual. He wondered what it would be like kissing her. He would never know. All because of some arrowhead he'd found in the woods. Why had he even picked it up? He should have stuck to plastic eyeballs.

IN
DA
BASEMENT

By the time the cake was served, Emma had become the center of attention. Not only was Kelly flirting with her, but now Courtney and Sienna Jones were asking her questions about being the new baseball star. Emma didn't know what else to do, so she ate her cake and tried not to talk too much. This made her seem even more mysterious to the girls, which made them like her more.

Once the birthday cake was finished, people began wondering when they would go to the basement. Jeff Matthews hadn't arrived yet. *Leave it to Jeff to try to make a grand entrance,* Emma thought. He was obviously coming late to impress everyone.

Kelly was not going to wait, though. At exactly six o'clock, she began herding her friends toward the stairs.

"We'll be watching the *Teenage Princess Fantasy* DVD, so don't disturb us," Kelly instructed her mother.

The Angstrom basement was definitely Make-Out Central. It was warm and cozy. The lights were dimmed. Comfy couches were arranged so they faced each other. Emma really liked the thick red carpet and the huge home theater center. All the girls piled onto one couch, and the boys plopped down on another. Kelly pulled the coffee table close between them. A large closet across the room was decorated with streamers. They all stared at it. This was probably where the actual kissing would happen.

Then things got even more interesting. Jeff came strutting down the steps wearing a new-looking Brooklyn Beats sweatshirt, a white visor, and bright yellow Etnies skate shoes. Even though Emma remembered her glimpse of the "real" Jeff during art class, she couldn't control how her heart skipped a beat when she saw him. He was still one of the cutest boys in her school, and he knew how to make himself the center of attention.

"Whasssuuuuup, my par-tay people?" Jeff said loudly. He high-fived some of the boys.

"We're waitin' for you, dawg!" Zach said.

"Who's ready to get their groove on?" Jeff asked, surveying the room with an expectant smile.

Kelly smiled back, tossing her hair behind her shoulder. She'd had her groove on since second grade, Emma decided.

"Are you ready to play the finest kissing game in the land?" Kelly asked the girls, who began to whisper and laugh.

"People, she's talking about Seven Minutes in Heaven!" Jeff said.

Emma was getting *very* anxious. The fourth day was almost over. How were she and Tom going to get away from the others? They needed to do something—and fast.

TOM GETS MASSIVELY DISSED BY KELLY

Tom was the only girl not falling off the couch with excitement. He watched while Jeff handed out paper and pencils.

"Put a kiss on them, ladies," Jeff laughed. "And guys, try not to drool on them too much."

Tom rolled his eyes as the other girls scribbled down their names. "I'm using a bigger piece of paper," Courtney whispered to Sienna. "I want to get picked first."

"I'm folding mine." Rachel smiled, revealing her heavy braces. "That way it sticks out more."

Sienna handed Tom a pencil. "Here ya go, Emma."

Tom reluctantly wrote *Emma Baker* on one of the slips of paper. He did not like how this was going, and he was not—under *any* circumstances—going to kiss a boy.

When everyone had written his or her name, Jeff placed the pieces of paper in two shoe boxes—one for the boys and one for the girls. Then he shook the closed boxes over his head. He did a little hip shimmy for the girls while they waited. But Tom could tell by the bored looks on the girls' faces that they were tiring of the Jeff Matthews show. They wanted him to hurry up and draw some names.

Actually, everyone seemed pretty distracted, so Tom moved off his couch and snuck over to Emma. "We gotta get out of this," he whispered to her.

"I know," she whispered back.

But Courtney got between them. "You guys have to wait your turn just like everyone else!"

"Yeah," Rachel added. "You already had your closet time with Tom. Give someone else a chance!"

Everyone laughed at that. Tom returned to his seat and Emma gave him a helpless look.

Suddenly everything stopped. Someone had opened the basement door. "Kelly?" Mrs. Angstrom was coming down the steps. "We still have some soda up here. Do people want popcorn?"

"Mom!" Kelly cried. "What are you doing? We don't need anything right now!"

"I put some popcorn in the microwave in case you want some during the movie."

"We don't."

Jeff slipped the shoe box under the coffee table. A couple of the boys snickered.

"Last chance," Mrs. Angstrom said. The buttery smell of popcorn wafted through the basement.

"That smells killer," said one of the boys. A few of the others looked hopefully toward Kelly.

Kelly had no choice but to stand up. "Fine," she said. "Who wants to help me bring down popcorn?"

Sienna and Rachel volunteered. Tom decided he wanted to help out too—five minutes next to Kelly was worth the trouble of ditching one of his crutches and balancing a bowl of popcorn in one hand. As he followed the other girls, Emma tried to go with him, but Courtney grabbed her. "No way. You're staying right here with us!"

Tom hobbled upstairs with Rachel and Sienna. Mrs. Angstrom had set up trays of popcorn, potato chips, and dip on the kitchen table. Everyone took something to carry down to the basement. When Tom picked up a bowl, Kelly grabbed his arm.

"What are you doing?" she snapped. "Don't touch that!"

Tom stepped back. As long as he was in Emma's tiny body, Kelly was a real threat. "But I just want to help."

"Well, don't," Kelly said. She gave Tom the nastiest look he'd ever seen. "And by the way, I'm sick of hearing about you and Tom in the janitor's closet. It doesn't matter anyway, because *I* like him now, and he likes me. I don't want you getting in the way, do you understand?"

Tom gulped. "But we're just friends." Kelly had to be kidding. She wouldn't actually threaten somebody, would she?

Kelly crossed her arms. "Everyone knows you like him."

"They do?"

"But that's over. Like I said, he likes me now. And we all

know that there are certain things that I have"—she pointed at her chest—"that you don't."

Tom couldn't believe what he was hearing. "You think Tom's going to like you because you have bigger—"

"Actually, I *know* Tom will like me better. That's how guys are. And since you're kind of *lacking* in that department, I guess you're outta luck." She snatched the bowl of dip from his hands. "I don't know why you even came here. No boy would want to kiss you anyway."

What a witch, Tom thought, as his fantasies of Kelly went down the toilet. Slowly, he limped back downstairs. He was just in time for the first drawing. Ashley had drawn the names and handed them to Jeff. "First up," he announced, "are Tom Witherspoon and Rachel Simms!"

"Armpit Breath herself," Brad said behind his hand. The boys snickered.

Rachel grabbed Emma's hand.

"I can't," Emma pleaded. "I'm not ready. I'm passing on this round."

Jeff laughed. "There's no *passing.*"

There was no stopping Rachel either. She pulled Emma toward the closet.

"Why is Rachel first?" Kelly grumbled from the couch.

"Hey, I just read the names. Everything else is the luck of the boxes," Jeff said, grinning.

"Stop complaining," Sienna said. "You'll get your turn with Tom."

"I'll complain if I want!" said Kelly. "Anyway, Rachel smells."

Meanwhile, Tom and the others watched Emma try to escape. "But you don't want to kiss me, I have chapped lips," Emma told her.

"I don't care," Rachel said stubbornly. The girl could not take a hint.

"And I, uh, have terrible breath. I just ate an onion garlic sandwich."

"Stop stalling!"

"And I have a rash. It's contagious!"

"We only have seven minutes!"

Tom remembered when Emma had scared off Zach Leland. He thought of Emma acing his tryouts and getting him on the A team. Even the day they switched, she hadn't told Mrs. Weissman that he was on the trampoline. She had been totally cool about it.

Then he thought all the way back to fourth grade, when he and Emma built the tree fort. He remembered the night when they slept under the stars and how he had watched her sleep and promised himself he would always look out for her and protect her.

This seemed like the right time to make good on that promise.

EMMA ESCAPES, JUST BARELY

Emma was fighting for her life in the closet. Rachel had pushed her inside and was trying to shut the door. Emma kept blocking it with her foot, but that just made Rachel slam it harder.

"C'mon, Tom, I know you like kissing girls," Rachel said when she finally got it closed. She pressed up against Emma, her lips inches from Emma's face.

Emma tried to squirm away.

"What's the matter? You kissed Emma. What's wrong with me?"

"But I didn't kiss Emma. I really didn't."

"Then I'll be your first!"

"But what about Grrlzillas?" Emma pleaded. "And when I looked under Margaret's skirt. Remember how mad at me you were then?"

"That is *soo* in the past."

"But that was Tuesday!"

"Things have changed. We've *grown*."

Emma tried to shift herself out of Rachel's kissing range, but a vacuum cleaner hose was sticking her in the butt.

"C'mon. We'll go slow if you're nervous."

Emma felt Rachel moving toward her in the dark. She could smell her famous death breath closing in. . . .

And then a little miracle happened.

The door swung open. Light burst into the darkness. A hand reached in and grabbed Rachel by the wrist and yanked her out of the closet. Then Tom stepped in and closed and locked the door behind him.

"Thank God!" Emma was so grateful that she threw her arms around his tiny girl body and squeezed. Tom hugged her back. But now what could they do?

Just then they heard Rachel's whiny voice. "Emma totally cut!" she cried. "Right in the middle of our kiss!"

"That little brat!" Kelly said. There was a loud knock on the door. "Emma Baker, you come out here this second. I don't care if you're on crutches. This is my party, not yours!"

"Now what do we do?" Emma asked.

"I don't know. But I'm not going out there. She's out for blood."

"But we have to do something. And we can't lose any more time."

"No way. I'm not getting beaten up by a girl."

Emma squeezed his hands. "Not even sexy Kelly Angstrom? The hottest girl in our class?"

"Doesn't matter. I'm not doing it."

"Yeah," said Emma. "You're probably right. It would be terrible having that curvy body mashing into you, having to smell that beautiful hair of hers. She'll probably have to sit on you. She'll probably have to *straddle* you. She'll probably have to use her whole body to hold you down. . . ."

"Fine," he snapped. "I'll do it, but only because we have to. And you have to help."

They opened the door. The minute the birthday girl saw Tom, she lunged for him. She dragged him out of the closet and tackled him onto the carpet.

"Wow," Zach Leland cheered. "Emma versus Kelly. This is like mud wrestling!"

Everyone gathered around to watch. Emma noticed that Tom actually managed to land a few good pinches and slaps. *Well,* thought Emma, *if Tom couldn't kiss Kelly Angstrom, getting beat up by her must be the next best thing.*

Then something landed on the floor. A rubbery jelly thing had fallen out of Kelly's shirt.

"What is that?" Courtney asked, peering at it.

"Did that come from Kelly's bra?" Ashley said.

Several of Kelly's shirt buttons had popped during the struggle, and people could see that there was another rubbery thing in the other cup of her bra.

"They look like fake boobs," Rachel said in disbelief.

"Well, they're not!" said Kelly. She tried to grab it back.

"I've seen these on infomercials," Hannah shrieked.

Ashley crossed her arms across her chest angrily. "But you already *have* breasts. You have the biggest in our class!"

"Why do you need more?" Hannah asked.

Rachel stared Kelly down. "Are you that greedy? Are you that fake?"

"That goes against everything Grrlzillas stand for!" Courtney cried.

"Grrlzillas?" Kelly snorted. "What a joke! What do I care about other girls? You losers just get in my way." She grabbed her fake boobs. "You guys can just leave right now!" And with that, she ran upstairs.

BACK IN
THE CLOSET

Now what was going to happen? Tom looked around for Emma. Was there still time to change back?

Courtney took charge. "Since our parents won't be here for another hour and we're stuck here anyway, I say we finish what we started. Who wants to keep playing Seven Minutes in Heaven?"

At first, no one said anything. The boys were still in shock over Kelly. Then Rachel raised her hand. Then Hannah. Brad and Zach followed. Soon everyone had his or her hand up.

Wincing, Tom got up from the floor and went to join the girls, but Courtney pulled him and Emma toward the closet. "Not you two," she said with a wink. "You guys still have five minutes left in the closet."

"But what about me?" Rachel protested. "Those are my five minutes!"

"Sorry, Rach," Courtney said. "Emma has earned this. She stood up to Kelly. Besides, something is obviously going on with them."

The other girls giggled.

If only you knew, Tom thought.

Back in the closet, Tom and Emma wasted no time. Tom turned the vacuum cleaner on its side so they could sit. Emma got out the arrowhead.

"Okay," she said. "This might be our last chance."

Tom began to sweat. "What exactly do we do?"

"Let's start with positive things. Things we've learned that have helped us understand the other person."

Tom scratched his head. He hated doing things like this. "Okay. Uh, well, I learned how to undo a bra."

"Be serious!"

"I am! That stuff is a big deal for girls."

Emma tried to stay positive. "Okay, well, I learned how important sports are to boys and why they take them so seriously. Spending time with their dads seems important too."

"That's true."

"Your turn now. Try holding the arrowhead with me. That might help."

As the two of them held hands, Tom closed his eyes and hoped they were only moments away from switching. "Um . . . okay. I learned that if you have too many activities, you turn into a little robot."

Emma frowned. "I'm not a little robot, Tom."

"You kind of are," Tom said. "I mean, I've been you for four days. I think I'd know."

166

"There you go again," Emma said sourly. "Is everything a joke to you?"

Tom didn't like the sharp tone in Emma's voice. "I'm trying to explain what I've learned about you."

"But that doesn't mean you're supposed to criticize. That's exactly what we're *not* supposed to do if we want to switch back."

"Well, what about you? You've criticized me the whole time we've been switched."

"How have I been criticizing you?"

"Telling me my friends are psychos, and that I'm a moron and a slacker."

"Well, you are a moron and slacker!"

"Well, then you're a robot!"

"At least I'm a successful robot."

"Who cares if you're successful? A robot is a robot."

Emma let go of Tom's hand. "This is never going to work. We haven't learned anything."

Tom shook his head. Emma sighed and pushed a button to light up her watch. "Anyway, it's now been four full days and a couple of hours. Even if we could stop arguing, we missed the deadline. It's over. We blew it."

Tom hung his head. This was definitely the worst day of his life.

Emma stuck the arrowhead back in her pocket. "So now what do we do?" she asked.

"We're screwed, I guess. We'll probably have to tell our parents."

"My mom will so freak out," Emma said. "She freaks out

167

if I buy a new skirt. Imagine what she'll do when I come home with a new body."

"My mother will have a nervous breakdown," said Tom. "She'll go insane."

"They'll probably send us to doctors and psychologists and stuff."

"I know," said Tom. "That's what they did when my parents got divorced."

"They won't let us take showers."

"I'll be banned from baseball. They won't even let me play *girls'* softball, because everyone will know I'm a boy."

They lapsed into a gloomy silence.

"Or else we could *not* tell people," Emma said softly.

Tom raised an eyebrow. "Do you think?"

"We'd have to always stay together," reasoned Emma. "In high school we'd have to be boyfriend and girlfriend. Then we'd have to get married. But we could do it. It's possible. Nobody would ever have to know."

"Yeah, but you'd be stuck with me," said Tom. "Could you stand being with a moron and a slacker all your life?"

Emma was quiet for a second. "I guess I could. I mean, it wouldn't be the easiest thing in the world. But I could."

Tom was surprised to hear her say that.

"Could you do it?" Emma asked.

"Sure. I mean, you're cool enough when you get right down to it. And everyone knows the dorky girls always turn out hot. You'll probably be like a supermodel someday. Oh wait, no, I guess it would be *me* who would turn into a supermodel."

"Would our kids be the right sex?" asked Emma. "Or would they be switched too?"

"I don't know."

They both thought about this. It all seemed strangely possible.

Then there was a noise outside. It was Brad and Rachel.

"I don't care!" Rachel was shouting. "I drew Tom and I should be in there with him!"

"But he's with Emma!" said Brad.

"But he's supposed to be with me!"

Tom and Emma stood up. Rachel must have found a key, because the door suddenly swung open. Rachel stood before them, Brad still trying to hold her back.

"Tom! *Tom!*" she cried. She grabbed Emma and tried to pull her out of the closet. Tom tried to yank Emma back in.

Brad was still holding on to Rachel. "You heard Courtney! Leave them alone and close the door!" Brad jerked Rachel backward. Then he lifted his leg and slammed the door with his foot.

This was bad timing. Tom and Emma were both leaning forward to see what was happening. The door hit them both in the face and forehead. A blinding red flash exploded in Tom's head. Somewhere he could still feel Emma beside him, and he tried to break her fall. Then he tumbled into the closet and everything went black.

HEAVEN ON EARTH

When Emma opened her eyes, the room was still spinning. Courtney and Ashley hovered over her. She felt like she'd just ridden the Wild Thing Roller Coaster at Wild Waves.

"What is up with you guys?" Courtney said, pulling her to a sitting position. "If you were so in love, why didn't you tell somebody?"

Tom was waking up too. Emma watched him try to lift his head, but it seemed like he could barely move. Emma blinked. Wait a minute. What was she seeing? She looked down at her body. Instead of cargo pants and muddy sneakers, she had on her favorite jeans. A cute T-shirt. And her ankle was bandaged—and sore.

She stared as Tom crawled over to her. "Are you okay?" he whispered into her ear.

"We're us again!" she whispered back excitedly. "I'm me—in my body!"

Tom had a crazy grin on his face. He patted his crotch. "It's there!"

Emma clutched her chest, then breathed the biggest sigh of relief in the world. "Same with me!"

That was when they both realized everyone at the party was staring at them.

But it didn't matter.

The curse was broken.

GENDER BLENDER

The gender reports were due Monday morning. Tom was still finishing his while Ms. Andre made announcements. Fortunately, she didn't call on Tom first, or even Emma. Instead, she asked Brad to get things started, with Margaret to follow. He took his paper to the front and faced the class.

"Some things I learned about girls from Margaret Cooper," Brad began, shuffling his feet. "Number one. Girls are not as nerdy as you think. Margaret had some excellent computer games, including Halo Two and Ghost Recon Three. She also had some old dolls, and she let me blow them up with firecrackers. This one doll's head went flying all over her backyard.

"Another thing I noticed about Margaret is she is very worried you're going to punk her. She's always checking behind her. I don't think boys worry about this as much. They understand that getting a wedgie or having someone pull your gym shorts down is actually a bright spot in an otherwise boring existence. I think that is an example of society and gender and things like that.

"Overall, doing this assignment with Margaret wasn't as bad as I thought. Mainly because she spent most of the time hiding in the bathroom whenever I came over."

When Brad finished, he took a little bow. Several girls booed on Margaret's behalf.

Margaret got up from her seat and walked to the front of the room. She took a deep breath. "Spending time with Brad was pretty much the worst thing that ever happened to me. But since my mother always tells me to look at the bright side, there were some good things too.

"One good thing he did was fix the chain on my bike. So it's true that boys can fix things. He also showed me how to open the lock on my sister's diary. Then he figured out how to disconnect the garage-door opener so my dad can't put his car away. I told Brad I didn't want to disconnect the garage door but he didn't listen and he did it anyway. My dad got very mad.

"Brad really only cares about three things: video games, breaking into things, and drawing naked girls. I told him if he drew a picture of me I would kill him, but of course the minute I said that, he drew one and showed it to everyone. My main thought after doing this assignment with Brad is I wonder if there are still convents and nuns because maybe I could join one."

Ms. Andre didn't seem very pleased. There was some

uncomfortable shifting of chairs as Margaret returned to her desk, but otherwise, the room stayed quiet.

"Let's start with a boy this time," Ms. Andre finally said. "Tom?"

Tom scribbled down one last thing, then walked slowly to the front of the class, bumping into a chair along the way. He was still getting used to being back in his body.

"Being with Emma Baker over the last week has shown me how complicated things are for girls. They have more rules than boys do, and people expect more of them. People figure boys are just going to run around and smash things up, and that's okay because that's how boys are. But girls are supposed to be more responsible and civilized.

"There is a lot more pressure on girls to look right and be liked by everyone. Some girls are really competitive and mean." He looked straight at Kelly when he said this. She was busy doodling in her notebook. "Girls have to be very smart about people. If they have a problem with someone, they have to think about who is friends with that person and who is friends with the friends of that person. Or like, if someone accuses a girl of something, she can't just fight that person and have it settled. She has to live it down somehow and prove to everyone she didn't do it.

"But even with all the stuff she has to deal with, Emma is always super-nice to people, even to boys. That's part of the reason she can handle so much. She's a good example of how a straight-A activities dork can actually be a really cool person in the end."

Tom snuck a glance at Emma. She was looking down at

her report, trying to act casual, but Tom could tell she was secretly really pleased. She slid out of her seat and went up to the front.

"One thing I learned from Tom over the last week was that being a boy can be lonely. They're supposed to be tough and cool around their friends. But at the same time, they have family problems and girl problems and a lot of feelings to deal with. The trouble is, no one teaches them how to deal with all these things.

"Girls are especially difficult for them because they think they're supposed to act like they don't care about us. But really they do. They want to be honorable and do the right thing, because in their secret way they want to protect us and be there for us. This is one of the deepest feelings they have.

"But they don't think they can show it. If you are a boy and you show weakness, you lose at the game of life. So boys have to keep everything inside.

"Which leads me to the main thing I learned. Boys and girls are not as different as you think. Sure, they dress and act different, and society says they should do different things. But in the end, they just want to be loved. They want to have good friends, and people to care about, who will care about them. We are all just trying to deal with our problems and do the right things and have a good life. Even people who pull down other people's pants, *Brad*."

The whole class burst into laughter, especially Tom. Who knew Emma could be so funny? Tom looked over at a grinning Ms. Andre. She definitely seemed impressed by their essays.

The bell rang and everyone rushed out. But Ms. Andre called Tom and Emma back to her desk. Ms. Andre studied their faces carefully as they stood before her.

"I don't think I've ever heard anything quite like your reports."

Tom shrugged. Emma smiled.

"How did you come so far in one week?"

"Just luck, I guess," Tom said.

"We were friends before," Emma said. "So we kind of knew each other."

"Still, those were very special reports," Ms. Andre said.

"Yeah," Tom said. "We've kind of always been in each other's heads."

"We're practically brother and sister," added Emma.

"Or something," Ms. Andre said, still amazed.

"Or something," Tom agreed.

BOSS OF THE TREE FORT

That afternoon when Emma got home, her mother wanted to talk.

"You've been acting different," Mrs. Baker said as they sat down at the kitchen table.

No kidding, Emma thought.

"Everything that's gone on this past week—slouching in your chair, staring off into space, sticking tape on the cat, telling Claire off. You've been acting like, well, a teenager," Mrs. Baker said.

Tom put tape on my cat? Emma thought angrily.

"And your gymnastics meet," continued Mrs. Baker. "I thought you'd be devastated, but in fact you seemed distracted, like you had more important things on your mind."

"I guess—I guess I've been thinking about a lot of

things lately," Emma said truthfully. "My life has been pretty stressful."

Her mom took her hand. "I realize that, honey. And that's not good. I ran into Tom Witherspoon's mother the other day and we started talking. We were both struck by how quickly your lives are changing. And how much we still want to be a part of them."

"Mmm," Emma said, wondering what her mom would say if she knew the truth.

"I don't know what's happening, but I do feel like . . . well, I feel like you're growing up," her mom went on. "And it's probably time for you to start making some of your own decisions, like Claire does. So your dad and I had a chat, and we feel that if you want to cut back on your after-school activities and have more time to yourself, that's up to you."

Emma's mouth fell wide open. Her parents were being more understanding than ever!

"Sound good?" Mrs. Baker asked.

Emma impulsively reached over and hugged her. "Sounds great."

And so that afternoon, Emma didn't do extra-credit homework, go to Girl Scouts, or practice her finger exercises for piano lessons. Instead, she went outside and found Tom, who was working on the tree fort.

"Hey!" she called to him. "Can I come up?" She had something with her too, something to make the tree fort extra-special.

"Sure."

"What are you doing up there?"

"I'm building a new hatch with a better lock. You can't threaten to pee on eighth graders without expecting payback."

Emma carefully climbed up the ladder and sat beside him. "But it'll be summer soon. . . . Won't they forget about it?"

"If someone almost peed on your head, would *you* forget about it?" Tom asked.

"I guess not," Emma admitted. She picked up a screwdriver and helped Tom tighten the screws.

They worked quietly for a while. It was a beautiful spring evening. The sun was going down, and the air smelled of apple blossoms and freshly cut grass. Tom couldn't have been more relieved that things were back to normal. In fact, he felt like they were even better than normal. Ricky had left his new baseballs alone. His mother seemed happier. His father was taking him to a Mariners game next weekend. And he and Emma were friends again.

"Hey, Emma, I've been meaning to ask you," he said. "Would you really have stayed with me forever if we never switched back?"

"I would have tried," Emma said.

"But wouldn't that have made you crazy?"

"Maybe," said Emma. "But I might have driven you crazy too."

"Yeah," said Tom. "With all that crap in your shower. Exfoliating Sensitizer!"

"All that crap in my shower?" Emma laughed. "You had more crap in your *pockets* than I had in my whole house!"

"Well, at least I had stuff a person might need. Your backpack had a whole library in it! Like you could ever read all that junk."

"It's called *homework?*" Emma said. "And talk about useless junk—have you seen the inside of your locker lately?"

Tom smirked. "Yeah—you cleaned it out. Now I can't find anything!"

"Like what? A week-old bologna sandwich?" Emma asked.

"I was still eating that!"

Emma replied with a deep sigh. And then she wagged a finger at him. "And I can't believe you put tape on my cat!"

"What? No, I didn't."

"Yes, you did."

"I did not."

"My mother saw you!"

"Cats happen to like it when you put tape on them."

"They do not!"

Tom rolled his eyes as he finished with the hatch and moved on to the next thing: a new piece of carpet for the floor. Emma had brought it from her basement. Tom laid it on the floor and unrolled it.

"This is the carpet you brought?" he asked, staring at it.

"Yeah," Emma said. "Is something wrong?"

"It's *pink.*"

"No, it's not. It's rose."

Tom frowned. "This is a tree fort," he said. "You can't have a rose carpet."

"Why not? We need some lighter colors. Everything else up here is brown or green."

Tom looked at her. "Hello? Tree *fort!* Are you not hearing the word *fort?*"

"Well, so what?" Emma said. "A fort can have something pink in it."

"Yeah, maybe on planet Wuss. But not here."

Emma smoothed it with her hand. "I happen to think it looks good."

"Well, I happen to think it looks terrible."

"That's just your opinion."

"Well, I happen to be the boss of this tree fort."

Emma stared back at him. "Oh yeah?"

"Yeah."

"Was there a vote?"

"Yeah. I voted for myself and I won."

"What if I don't accept that?" Emma said.

"Doesn't matter. Boys are always the bosses of tree forts."

"That's ridiculous. Boys are too stupid to be the bosses of tree forts! Or anything else!"

"You're the one who didn't properly defend yourself. You had to *pee* on your attackers!"

"And what would you have done?"

"Not that!"

Just then a strong wind blew through the trees. Leaves and pine needles rained down all around them. Tom and

Emma looked up at the sky, which was starting to grow dark.

"You did get rid of that arrowhead, didn't you?" Emma asked nervously.

Tom nodded. "I gave it to the Seattle Historical Society. They said they'd put it in their collection."

Emma watched the sky. "Just to be safe, let's not argue."

"Good idea."